Sophia von X

Victoria Ray

CHAPTER 1

LEAVING THE NEST

Sabina parked the car by the roadside. She gathered her bag, shrugged, and walked down the paved alley to the Meno Uno Café. It was January—the time when Sicily is wet and chilly. Usually, Palermo gets soaked with the fog and rain; tourist attractions and cafeterias are deserted. This winter wasn't an exception.

Sabina was cross, and it showed in her walk. This was meant to be the day that she took her beloved purple Peugeot, named Holmes, and traveled north into Germany to get away from her ex-husband and family. But her brother, Matteo, had picked today of all days to beg for a meeting. He told her on the phone that he wanted to talk about "some important business," and he wanted to meet, despite the fact that he didn't bother coming for Christmas and was too busy with his new 'Ndrangheta family.' It seemed he had finally found the time to badger her about the problems with Dario, her soon-to be ex-husband, if that's even why he wanted to talk.

Matteo was already waiting on the outdoor seating. He was

handsome, young, and well-groomed. He wore a fine woolen suit, elegant shoes from Antonio Mecariello, and a classic blue Borsalino hat. People always thought he was Sabina's twin, but she was in fact ten years his senior.

"Sabina! Why the frown, Love? I haven't seen you in two months!"

"That's why you get a frown, Matteo." The woman sat down and picked up the menu. "What were you thinking, not coming for Christmas? Mama was gloomy the whole time! It's just one weekend!"

"I was invited to Christmas with friends. I could hardly say no."

Sabina's family was well known in Sicily. Her father, Frank Ferrara, was the son of the last Etna vintner. After Frank married Maria, he borrowed money and founded a winery, *Sogno d'Amore.* He became fascinated with the wine world and tried to become the best in the field. Little by little, Frank and Maria began to purchase the lands in the neighborhood that had been abandoned. The complicity of the wine they produced led to a thousand visitors each year and better sales. *Sogno d'Amore* wines became the trademark of Sicily's flavor, lifestyle, and spirit. For many years, Frank tried to convince Matteo to continue the family business, but it seemed Sabina's brother never developed the passion for cultivating grapes or working with the soil.

"You know what? It doesn't even matter, but why now? Why outside, in a café?"

The waiter approached their table. "Ready to order? *Che cosa desidera?*"

Matteo smiled. "A caffe corretto, with sambuca."

"I'll have the roasted swordfish with tomatoes, olives, and capers. And a double espresso, please."

"Hungry? You always had a great appetite."

"I might as well eat while I'm here." Sabina looked up, waiting for her brother to stop the small talk.

"I heard you filed for divorce from that deadbeat. About time."

"I did. And I meant what I said in my texts: don't hurt him, or...don't kill him. Just let him be."

The waiter interrupted them again. "Your drinks. The order is on the way."

When he left, Matteo continued, "Kill? Girl, I'm not some American gangster from a movie," he shot the air wildly with his fingers. "I was just going to bruise him. You've always said, 'only when he leaves me, Matti'..."

"I was joking, silly boy! This isn't funny! I want—*need*—to move on, and having Dario in the hospital won't help. I'd probably come back to stand by his bedside. Let the past be the past, brother. I'll go on my holiday, and you keep your nose clean. Okay?"

Matteo grinned while anger gleamed in his dark eyes. "Are you protecting him? That dumbass was hitting you! I think he's got it coming."

Sabina sighed and followed the movements of the waiter who had arrived with a fish plate. She didn't want to continue, but she knew her brother too well.

"You know what, Matti? Maybe I'll change my mind later, but I'm pretty fragile and tired right now. Could you, please, not bring more violence into my life?"

Matteo's face melted. For a moment, he looked sweet and boyish again.

"Fine. Maybe revenge is a dish best served cold, unlike that fish on your plate. I wish I ordered too."

Sabina touched his hand, laughing. Matteo continued in another vein.

"What's this I hear about you leaving your job at the university? You fought so hard for it as I remember!"

"I'm taking paid leave. They've forced me to. Look, at the end of the year, I was going through hell with Dario. I was a complete mess! They had to hire a secondary teacher, Ucko Lifebelt," she paused. "I'll be back next year."

"Alright. Where are you going?"

"I haven't decided yet," Sabina lied. "Somewhere off of the island."

"Why leave? Go see the Valley of Temples or climb Etna."

Sabina laid her cutlery on the empty plate and looked straight into her brother's eyes, making a point that the conversation was over.

"Okay, I see you're in a rush. Just be good to yourself, my little sister." Matteo loved to pretend he was older. Sabina's youthful looks let it work more often than not.

"I'll call you when I get wherever I'm going, big brother."

They paid and then walked together down the alley, passing a silent, bearded man huddled in a black coat. He raked his eyes up and down Sabina's body as if to criticize the bright yellow dress she wore. She shivered. Her ex-husband, Dario, wore a beard too, which is why bearded men had now made her feel unsafe.

As soon as she was nestled in the driver's seat of her beloved tiny Holmes, Sabina felt a thrill of excitement. She had lied to Matteo. She knew exactly where she was going, Bingerbruck, Germany, to visit the unique, recently discovered holy tomb of Christianity. Being a teacher of philosophy and a Catholic, she had found the new burial site fascinating and disturbing. Media reports had made astonishing claims, some of which she had already heard in the past ten years. Others, though, couldn't even be imagined. Sabina knew about the ideas of the Greek philosopher Celsus, who thought Jesus's father was a soldier named Panthera. She recalled that his grave was found in Bingerbruck in 1859. Now, in 2017, they had uncovered a fresh, unusual vault not far from Panthera's grave, which bore the numbers 22:12. Last week, the authorities confirmed that it was a reference to the text from the *Book of Revelation*.

Behold, I'm coming soon! My reward is with me, and I will give to each person according to what they have done.

They said it was apparent—the tomb belonged to someone from Jesus's family (probably his brother or a child), who had chosen to be buried near Panthera. Theological magazines described the findings in detail. It had been covered in marble cladding with a bronze cross carved into the surface of the tomb, just like the previous one. In addition, researchers from the National Scientific Team of Germany confirmed a new element on the site—a small window cut into the limestone wall.

Sabina understood that archaeologists had discovered thousands of such tombs around the world. Each one had a history behind the burial place and reliable evidence about Jesus being a soldier or a builder. The gospels specify that Jesus was buried outside of Jerusalem, so who did those chambers with long niches, crosses, clothes, and bones belong to? The latest technology—DNA—would stop all doubt and give some much-needed evidence to the world of believers.

This last notion in the media—that Jesus was not the son of God, but a liar and warrior—jarred Sabina's heart the most. *How could the Prince of Peace be a man of deception and war?* She didn't know what she expected to find at the grave, but she felt that she would regret it if she did not go.

· · ·

Sabina drove through Palermo. It was her home, her birth town, an exquisite blend of Greece, Italy, Arabia, France, and Spain. It was an old city with new ways, the zone on the edge of Europe, the heart of the dangerous world. Still, each time she drove through, she enjoyed the views of the Church of Martorana, Piazza Pretoria, and the Castello a Mare Park. Palermo was the nest that had raised and shaped her, and finally she was ready to spread her wings.

Sabina traveled eastwards along the north coast, with the Tyrrhenian Sea dominating the horizon, until she arrived at the sea-sprayed docks about two-and-a-half hours later. She drove her purple Holmes onto a ferry and stood by the railing. A cold wind whipped her long, dark hair as the ferry slowly ploughed its way to the Italian mainland. Excitement ran through Sabina's mind and body. No one ever believed she could do it, but look at her now...She felt a quirky pride as she drove slowly off the ferry and onto the docks of Molo Beverello, Napoli. It was lunchtime, but Sabina was too enthusiastic to stop and eat. She headed north, towards the heart of Italy, a new Corsair headset on, listening to her favorite opera, Turandot.

The road passed small villages, fields, wine estates, tourist attractions—familiar in their similarity, but different enough to be interesting. A few hours later, even passion and music couldn't distract Sabina from her hunger. She turned off from the main road and followed the sign leading to a cozy town called Segni, located on a hilltop in the Lepini Mountains. The first place she spied was a hole-in-the-wall with the letters 'GREEN BAR' above the door. There was no parking. Sabina turned down the narrow street next to the church of Chiesa di S. Pietro. She saw a lot of cars that had been parked half up on the sidewalk. She followed their example. *Why not?* Sabina was so distracted grabbing her bag and coat and locking the car, that she didn't notice a pair of men until they were almost on top of her. The older guy was bearded with a much-abused cheap jacket. He smiled, showing smoke-yellowed teeth.

"Salve! You're a tourist, no? Maybe we can show you around. I think we should!"

Sabina's alertness sharpened to a knife's edge. She realized there was no one around: the place was lifeless. *What bad luck —a hungry, tired woman against two rough men in this rusty cross-section of alleys.* They carried with them a subtle air of casual menace that tied a knot in her stomach. The man with a wild beard looked her over with a lazy, entitled eye.

When Sabina spoke, her voice quivered. "I'm fine. I'm heading to a bar I saw on the street..."

"No need for that, sweet candy," the second man looked through the window of her car. "We know a better place nearby!"

He stepped up to her, still smiling. Sabina wanted to run, but she knew he'd grab her. She could scream, yes, she could, but her whole being was too terrified of what they'd do if she did. She stood frozen.

'The wild beard' casually reached for her handbag, whispering, "Let's find a better parking spot, yeah?"

"You know, guys," the firm, slightly tense voice seemed to come from nowhere. "I don't think the lady cares for your company!"

Three heads turned to look at the sound, equally surprised. It seemed like the guy had just appeared from the air, but as he closed his car door, Sabina realized he'd been in his car the whole time. He was sitting and watching them!

The man was small and bald, with a short red beard, his

arms covered with eclectic tattoos. He wasn't dressed for the chill, just wearing jeans and a black tee. The newcomer walked casually up to the wild beard, who stepped forward to meet him.

"You've got nerve! We happen to know little Miss here. Why don't you just f-u-..."

The short guy in a black tee jumped up and drove his bald head into the bearded man's face with a horrible crunch. The big fella collapsed on the ground, clutching at the blood gushing from his nose. Sabina hurried away towards the bar, shaking. Glancing back, she saw that the man from the car was following her, while the second attacker was helping his friend.

The tattooed man walked next to her, wiping the blood from his head, grinning: "I know what you're thinking. He's probably no better than them, right?"

All Sabina wanted was to get to the safety of the bar. She kept hurrying.

"I'm an ex-prize fighter, see? It's kind of in my blood. Men like those you met at the parking only speak one language. Do you know what I mean?" he continued.

"Thanks, really," Sabina said, still shaking. But here it was —the door, the long-awaited security.

The tattooed man gestured for her to go first, and then came in after Sabina. He jogged behind the bar to lean on the other side.

"Food? Drink? What will it be, Miss?"

Sabina stared at him for a minute, then started laughing: "Food. Oh God, thank you, I didn't mean to be rude!"

"I'm glad I was there. Don't worry, I'll walk you back to your car later, me or whomever you like..." He nodded at a towering lad serving sandwiches and beers to some locals.

"Thanks, I'd like that. I'll have a turkey sandwich and a double espresso," she said, glancing at the menu above the bar.

"Just passing through?" the man asked when her espresso was ready.

"Yes, I'm heading up to Bingerbruck. It's a holiday trip, not a very well planned one," Sabina explained.

"Sounds great! I used to travel, but not so much these days. I've got my baby here now." He gestured at his bar. Sabina was taking it all in. The walls were dark stained wood with matching tables, the bar—exquisite carved green marble.

"Very cool place."

"Isn't she?! I've wanted this bar for years!" He ran a hand over the marble, "but I could only afford it two months ago. I also run a gym in town, mostly for boxing and self-defense. You know, if you've got the time, I could show you how to deal with *testa di cazzo* like those two thugs."

"Me? No, I can't fight."

"Exactly! But a little training goes a long way." Seeing her discomfort, he held up his hands, "Just saying...if you change your mind. What's your name?"

"Sabina. Yours?"

"Luca."

After finishing a meal, Sabina let Luca walk her back to her car. She thanked him one more time and drove back up to the highway. She loved the feeling of being on the road. She felt God's presence by her side—His guidance, His warmth, His love. Knowing she was not alone made her life easier—to breathe, to live, to deal with violence and disorder in her marriage. God was the one who supported her through the dark side of life, through all disappointments and failures. She learned that the greatest enemy of joy was not her imperfections, but the constant demand of being perfect or flawless.

The confusing mystery of life was accepting the imperfection of everything that surrounds us. This was the only true wisdom.

When Sabina's car got to A1, and the land spread out around her, she understood how late it was. *No problems,* she thought. *I'm protected by Christ. He is the road, the guide, and the truth.*

CHAPTER 2

LIFE IS NOT FAIR OR MEETING GRACE

SABINA ROSE LATE, having slept till noon. The staff at Amati Residences served her free breakfast—a cappuccino and a buttery croissant—just as the billboard had advertised. After that, fuelled by small talk, smiles, delicious chocolate, and tiny sandwiches from roadside stops, she drove all the way to Switzerland. The view of cold mountains filled the northern horizon. With the sun dipping in the west, she passed the border, pulling into a very modern looking B&B, which was clean and pleasant. Sabina ate the standard Swiss dinner, consisting of soft bread, butter, cheeses, cold cuts, jam, and honey and talked politics and religion with an old Irish couple who was traveling to their grandson's wedding. The couple's opinion of the new grave was that it was:

1. at best—a mistake in archaeology.
2. at worst—lies, crafted to further faltering careers.

Sabina remained neutral. She didn't know the truth but wanted to. In her eyes, the truth was always something infinite, alive, not bound by human views or limits. The truth was The Way, hiding behind the distortion of the world, rational design of the Universe, or how we perceive our lives. If the tomb was a revelation of truth, then she had to *enter* it, without any help. She had to go beneath the sacred meanings, foolish traditions, supernatural suggestions, and subjective experiences.

Sabina went outside to be greeted by fresh snow. Switzerland was very different from her home island. In Sicily, it was very hard to find open space without running into more ancient walls or structures. Here in Switzerland, the civilization seemed to huddle by the roadside—everywhere she looked, she saw only wild naked mountains. Sabina felt more tranquil, less fighting within herself. She enjoyed being a tourist.

By lunchtime, she found herself driving through a massive valley surrounded by tended parks and a mingle of shops. She turned to an open Plaza that she had spotted before on the map. *Time to buy a warmer coat*, she thought to herself. Sabina browsed through clothing shops. The people were aggressively friendly. She ended up shaking hands with every shopkeeper and was trying to get used to saying 'hello' to every soul she passed. It was a bit intimidating, but also inclusive: it was hard to feel alone here.

Dressed in a new leopard faux fur coat and a woollen beanie, Sabina walked back towards her car. A young, thin man in jeans and a black jacket suddenly ran at her and swung to grab her handbag. *What? Again?* She stumbled back reflexively, hugging her purse, making him miss it. The guy dashed past, but only to grab another woman's satchel. The shocked woman fell on the ground. The man sped onward, dodging through the foot traffic. A suited older man yelled after him. Another guy, almost a kid, tried to trip the thief but missed.

Sabina was stunned. She tried to approach the victim, a young lady with pink hair and bold, green-rimmed glasses.

"Stop! No, fuck! Somebody stop him! He's got my bag!" The girl shouted in oddly accented English. She looked around for help, then ran after the man. Sabina felt very afraid for the girl chasing that man alone down the street. She followed her, first trotting, then forced to run—something she realized she hadn't done in a while.

The street was narrow, full of a jumble of bins, wrought iron stairwells, and parked scooters. At the far end, Sabina saw the girl turning down an empty street, desperately trying to catch the thief, but he had vanished. There were only shops, houses, cars sprawled in every direction, plus a couple of worried faces, heading about their business.

The girl began to howl. "My baaag, where is it?!?"

Sabina was breathing heavily from her sudden run. "It'll be okay...We can call the police..."

"You don't understand! I need that satchel. It's got my life's work in it. It's got my phone! The police will take too damn long!" The girl was in a panic.

Sabina understood the distrust of the police. Sicilians trusted no one—especially their leaders and those who served them.

"You said your phone?"

"Yes, my fucking phone!"

"We could track it, okay? Let's go to my car. We can use my laptop."

Ten minutes later, they sat in the warm embrace of the good-old Holmes. Sabina passed the girl her laptop. "I'm Sabina, and you?"

"Grace. Thanks a bunch, Sabina." She looked at the laptop, impatiently waiting for it to boot up.

"What is that accent?"

"Australian. I'm from, well...you would never have heard of where I'm from." she shot Sabina a nervous grin.

It took only a couple of minutes, with Grace swearing and drumming her fingers the whole time, before a Google account located the stolen phone, showing it neatly on a map—only three blocks away!

"We've got that cocksucker! Let's go, Sabina!"

"I think now is the time to call the police."

"Drive! Now!"

"Fine, but he could be dangerous. What then, Grace?" Sabina turned the key and started driving, feeling put-upon.

"I'll show him dangerous..." whispered Grace. The sound of abuse, aggression, and curse filled the air in the car. Sabina faced the rare glimpse of freedom in Grace's eyes. Freedom to endure, freedom to fight, freedom to die.

Sabina pulled up on the roadside. The laptop's indicator sat squarely in the house opposite them—a two-story tan stucco affair with a steep roof, wrought iron balcony, and an engraved door set with three triangles of glass. The door was wide open. Two young men stood on the patio, smoking.

Grace, with a red face and wild eyes, stepped out of the car, storming across the road. Sabina scrambled out after her. "Wait! Please, Grace, there's too many of them!"

Sabina could feel the cold fear running up her spine. Despite that, she jogged after the young Australian demon while wanting to move in the opposite direction. The two women contrasted, Sabina in a red flowing dress and leopard coat; Grace, with her pink hair, in warm tights printed with starfish, orange Doc Martens, and a large black windbreaker.

When the two young men saw Grace bash open the gate, one of them asked "*Je peux vous aider?* Can I help you? Are you Tyler's new girls?"

"I don't speak whatever that was." Grace stormed past, homing in on the loud ring tone echoing from inside. Sabina rushed behind her. The house was a mess. A bulky mongrel dog rose from a filthy bed. Grace spun around the next door-frame. The man was sitting on a stained couch with her satchel next to him. She saw her phone in his hand and a bemused expression on his face. Grace lunged at him, fingernails clawing straight into his eyes. The man howled in shock and pain, falling back on the bed, giving Sabina the time to snatch up her phone and satchel. He shouted and staggered up, cradling his face, eyes watering, blood on his fingers. It wasn't enough, no! Grace kicked him between the legs–full force! The man's face turned blue; he collapsed on the floor. The young Australian, full of rage, ran out of the house, past the two men who were still standing outside, absolutely shocked. Sabina felt uncomfortable, weak, and dumb, but she hurried after Grace, repeating, *please, forgive the sins of your servants, for we have been very foolish.*

The two women sat in a Crazy Cupcake café, eating sandwiches. They traded stories. They laughed. Sabina learned that Grace came from a coastal town called Batemans Bay, a tourist area, and had caught the travel bug. Grace told her that she had travelled around Australia, gone to Japan, flown to England, crossed to France, and was wandering around German and Switzerland now, deciding her next move from day to day. Sabina was a bit curious where the money came from because she knew how expensive it must be to travel. She couldn't help it though and found Grace's freedom infectious. By the end of their meal, Sabina had offered to take Grace north, as far as she wanted. The girl in orange Doc Martens accepted a new partner. Nothing unites people better than external circumstances, when their life is threatened or when they are the victim of another's aggression.

After driving three hours, Grace spotted a sign "The Rock Bottom Hotel" - one of its symbols indicated skiing opportunities. She pulled over and said, "This place looks perfect! It's got rooms, skiing, a sauna. I have to get out here. Don't worry, girl! I'll walk down…The map says it's only three clicks away."

Sabina blinked at her, surprised and hurt. "Are you sure? I don't understand. I thought we were traveling together now?"

"Sorry, my life is a path of exploration… It is about expanding the walls we are stuck in, about dealing with *now* and finding the divine in small corners of the world. My divine is here! I feel it. You've got my number anyway. Keep me posted about Bingerbruck, Babe!" With that, Grace gave her a thumbs up and headed off, with a cute bounce in her steps.

Sabina drove alone, thinking about all that had happened in the last few days. The roads were narrow and winding, with sudden cliffs and turns and almost no signage. She was afraid to fall asleep but couldn't find the right spot to stop. After thirty minutes of driving, she finally saw a cozy hostel, snuggled amidst the peaks on the brink of the Winterthur. *Good enough for a break! Tomorrow I'll be at the grave, the biggest discovery of the XXI century, face to face with the Holy Spirit and Jesus's family!* she thought while parking her purple Peugeot near the doors of Neuheji House.

The room number five was dark, humid, and full of snoring people. Sabina said her usual prayer, "To My God and All Things," preparing to sleep. On the floor, near the bed, she noticed a page from a notebook. Her curiosity took over—she picked it up, to read: *To turn from Everything to one face is to find oneself face to face with Everything.*

CHAPTER 3

THERE I SHALL COME TO MEET YOU

SABINA WAS glad when the winding mountain roads of Switzerland opened the view to a long highway that cleaved north to the German border. Swiss roads were beautiful but edged in cliffs. Despite this, no one seemed to feel the need for warning signs or safety barriers. No doubt, the love of adventure, risk, or danger, is located on the deepest level of the human psyche.

At the border, a stern German police officer examined Sabina's passport and driver's license. "Drugs? Alcohol? Dangerous liquids? Human slaves?"

"Only the Holy Spirit and prayers," answered Sabina.

"Don't you try to tempt me with your jokes, Miss!" The man scanned her tight dress, admiring the view of her curves. He looked a little bit like a Frankenstein's Monster or romantic Dracula, with eyes redder than blood, probably from the lack of sleep or alcohol abuse.

"The purpose of your visit, Miss Ferrara?"

"To see the world. My granny used to say…"

"I bet she did," the officer interrupted her with a bored smirk. "Where are you staying?"

"My address is one word–EVERYWHERE!" Sabina smiled.

The officer was confused. Was she making a joke, or was she serious? Women like this—candy-like, lonely, dark, with a trick-or-treat-kind-of-body— were too much trouble. He blinked and let her go, whispering to himself, "I think I know what you mean..."

The unfinished bottle of scotch was waiting inside of the warm border cabin. The officer went into the booth and made a quick call. "She's arrived."

Sabina pulled off the road at the foot of a low hill. It sat overlooking the Rhein, shrouded in snow-laden conifers. Through the trees at the hills bald top, she could make out tents, four-wheel drives, and the chaotic movements of people. Yes, she made it; the tomb was only a few steps away!

The phone rang. The caller ID had a picture of a grinning boy of eight holding a red toy sports car—her brother Matteo. She rolled her eyes and picked up.

"How's your holiday, sis?"

"It's going fine. I decided to see Germany. I'm visiting a famous castle right now."

"You drove through all Switzerland? Damn, I wouldn't brave those roads in the snow. Why didn't you take a plane?"

"Why are you calling, Matti? Has something happened?" Sabina was irritated.

"To see if you were okay! That's all. Dario is gone. I thought that prick followed you."

"No. Maybe he went to Tuscani to visit his family? Thanks

for the warning, but I've got to go. I've pulled over at the moment." Sabina wasn't too happy to think about her crazy ex, her little brother, or Sicily.

"Okay, Love. Take care."

Sabina climbed out of her car and shivered as a cold, chaotic, wind curled around her body. She pulled on her wool beanie, plunged hands a little bit deeper into her pockets, and trudged up the hill between the ancient trees. Sabina got a feeling that she saw a grey figure, right ahead, around the slope. She stirred into the darkness, but the shadow had vanished amidst the trunks. *Maybe there's someone else here to see the grave?* Sabina thought to herself. Nearing the crest, she could make out more details: two field tents were set up to one side of a small archaeological dig; several areas were being unearthed, but the excavation was uncovered. Two men tried to clear the place from the last snowfall. The third was sitting in the folding chair, checking his phone. As Sabina emerged from the trees, a rotund man picked himself up from a folding chair. He waddled towards her. As he got closer, she could see that he was in a security officer's uniform, with a license strapped in a transparent window on his arm.

"Stop! Who are you?" The big man spoke in heavily accented English.

"You people can't just waltz up here. This is private land!" He stopped, looming over her. His breath smelt awful.

What an odd man! What do I say now? Or do I just run? Sabina stared at his uniform near her nose, trying to think of an excuse to be here.

A deep melodic voice interrupted her thoughts. "It's alright, Bruno. She's with me."

Surprised, Sabina looked over to see a handsome man standing near the dig site. With irritation in his voice, the security officer said, "Well, Tom, you could have said that before I walked all the way over here!"

"Sorry, Bruno. My bad," her savior smiled, keeping his eyes on Sabina.

Bruno turned and stomped off towards the tent, swearing.

"Thanks for that," said Sabina.

"I thought it was my duty as a gentleman to save you from Bruno's halitosis. I'm Thomas von Essen. Who are you, and what brings you here?"

"Sabina Ferrara. I came to see the new grave. Do you think it has a connection to Jesus?"

Thomas nodded. "Yes, I think it has...People go nuts about this finding. Thank God the team here is very protective. Our Bruno has been turning everyone away."

Thomas lied: his real name was Thomas, but everything else—pure fiction. Being 'von Essen,' a part of a noble family with deep roots in Swedish and German royalty, was his biggest dream and the best cover-up story. That's why he was obsessed with the small details. Every little fact of his biography, every word of his jokes was carefully created, checked, tested out. The Essen name was a high-quality product with a high-quality tag. Thomas used it only in exceptional cases—in cases with a lot of money at stake.

"Who's running the dig? You?" Sabina asked after a pause.

"Well, that's a little complex. It's an international team of people with vested interests. Technically, the grey beard over there..." Thomas gestured at an old man in a coat, standing raven-like at the entrance of the field tent, "...is in charge. His name is Hermann Kushner-Parzinger, the president of the German Cultural Heritage Foundation."

"Why technically?"

"He's a bit cautious and easily cowed. There are a lot of dominant personalities around the world involved in this case. It's all about a collective vision and unified action, or so they say. Simply, there's been a lot of arguing how quickly, and with what methods, we should exhume the grave."

"Mmm, should I go? I mean, they'll figure out very soon that I'm not with you. They must know who's supposed to be here, right?"

"I'm *not* on their team." Thomas grinned.

"You're not?" Sabina started to feel suspicious.

"I represent the interests of a very powerful patron from Israel. He sent me here to get a first-hand record of this significant event. Mr. Kushner-Parzinger is happy enough to use my expertise as an archaeologist. Double luck!"

"What patron?" Sabina asked curiously. She was studying the handsome features of her company: Thomas was clean-shaven, with bright grey eyes and long blond locks. He reminded her of the melody maker, a man of art. His creativity shined through, mixing with excitement, hope, and doubts.

Thomas was silent. He walked towards the tents, then turned to the grave.

"I can hear you are Italian, Miss Ferrara," he said all of a sudden.

"Sicilian."

"A fascinating country and language–a woven tapestry of influences! And women, ah, the untouched, pure beauty," he murmured to himself.

They arrived at the dig site. Two men were sweeping up snow and depositing it in a wheelbarrow.

"Shouldn't all this be covered?" said Sabina, quizzically.

"Obviously. Last night the tent got vandalized. Beyond

repair, I'm afraid. The new tent is yet to arrive. As you can see, we're just trying to prepare the site for our professional teams to work without any disturbance," Thomas trailed off, squinting up at the sky. "Snow and wind! Again! Guys, everybody, cover the dig!"

The two men swore, clambered out of the shallow dig, and grabbed a large tarpaulin. They stretched it over the grave as flurries of snow began to swirl all around them. Everyone was hurrying for the shelter of the tents. Everyone...except for Thomas.

Sabina looked at him, perplexed. "Are we going to head inside, or no?"

"Not now," Thomas raised his voice over the snarling wind. "I think I'm going to have a look underneath to check if everything is alright. Please, stay here and tell me if anyone approaches." He started unpinning the canvas edge, taking a small peek inside.

"What? I don't understand. Why?" Sabina tried to stop him, but Thomas had already ducked out of sight, under the canvas. After a minute or two, Sabina heard the sound of something metallic repeatedly biting into the frozen soil.

What is he doing there? Does he just want to be the first to see it? He'll never find anything in this darkness. Sabina's mind was racing as she reluctantly stood guard.

Time ticked by. Sabina's only comfort was that the swelling storm worked well to conceal all sounds. The hammering stopped. Sabina grew tense.

"Mister von Essen? Are you okay? What's going on?"

The silence from the dig grew unbearable until Sabina decided to peek inside. She bent down...and then she saw *it*. Or him. On the other side, behind the trees, stood a grey figure, almost invisible through the snow. It reached into its jacket and took out a gun. Sabina couldn't see it clearly, but his gesture, the threatening extension of the arm were unmistakable. The sound of a gunshot cut through the snow. Sabina distinctly heard a whine as the bullet passed a hairbreadth from her ear. Fear gripped her body, shivering through each of her muscles like an electric shock. She felt light and dizzy. Her legs wanted to run, but that would leave Thomas alone and defenceless. The depth of that betrayal rooted her to the spot. Sabina ripped up the canvas in a panic. She met Thomas's eyes: he was looking up, bewildered. Somehow, he had not heard the gun!

"Killer!" Sabina shouted and then ran, screaming "help" as she heard another shot. Thomas scrambled out of the dig and fled with her. They ran down the slope, ducking under branches and dodging trees.

"Where are we going?" There was a hint of panic in Thomas's voice.

"Hooolllmmmeesss!"

"What!?"

"My car! It's his name!!"

A gunshot rang out again. Bark exploded off a tree next to Thomas. With a fearful glance back, he yelled, "Keep running! We are hard targets in this snow!"

Sabina saw Holmes taking form ahead of her, emerging from the whirling whiteness. She had never been more grateful for the keyless entry as she snatched open her door. Another gunshot. Sabina felt a searing pain, a yanking on her flesh at the top of the left shoulder. Her heart palpitated. She screamed.

Thomas stared at her in horror, whispering, "We'll die. We can't escape."

He continued to stare as she clambered into the car, hit the start button, lurched up onto the roadway, and roared away as fast as Holmes could go, recklessly ploughing through the snow. Thomas crouched down in the passenger seat.

When the distance from the hill stretched out, he asked, "Are you alright?"

"No! I just got shot! Who was that bastard? Tell me!"

"I don't know, Sabina. Someone is trying to interfere with the exhumation of the holy tomb. First, an expert from America was killed en route to the dig. She was meant to coordinate the team and head photography. She was found dead in the plane's latrine. Next, the tent, now...this."

"My shoulder hurts. I can't tell how much I'm bleeding. Can you check?"

"Do you have a first aid kit in the car?"

"In the glove box..."

"Great. Take two-three extra turns. Let's not make it easy for him to find us. When you get the chance, pull over."

Sabina turned off the road into an area of suburbs and pulled up by the side of an empty park. She started to pray, repeatedly chanting the words *My God, the divine rescuer.*

"Okay, girl. You are the rescuer today. You shed your precious blood for my salvation," Thomas winked. "Let's get those clothes off."

Sabina let him pull aside the shoulder of her dress, which was sticky with blood. Thomas craned his neck, examining the wound, and laughed.

"What? What is so funny?" Sabina was astonished and angered at the same time.

"It barely clipped you. The stain of sin on my soul has been cleansed. You are so lucky! It needs a couple of stitches, of course. It probably won't even scar. Look, I'll apply a dressing, then we'll get to a hotel, and I can give you the stitches there. Okay?" Thomas was smiling with relief.

Sabina frowned. "Are you a doctor? We should go to a hospital."

"I am not. I have a first-aid certificate. That's all. I do not recommend going to the hospital. First, there is only one near us. Second, that shooter knows he hit you. That means the hospital will be his next stop, Sabina. While he's looking for you there, we should be somewhere else entirely, don't you think?"

Sabina stared at Thomas's sincere smile, digesting what he had just said. She felt overwhelmed with guilt, rage, and sexual desire. She was a fallen creature in need of love and understanding. Erotic, almost animalistic images spiralled in her head.

"Do you believe in God, Mister von Essen?" she asked, preparing to give up.

"Of course. I am a man of faith who is searching for God." He whispered in her ear, "I am a believer...in exile."

Sabina couldn't hear his last words; she fainted with a smile on her face. Her soul had fully surrendered to the temptations of her heart. The darkness of our desires is the rent we pay for being humans.

CHAPTER 4

DARKNESS BORN FROM DARKNESS

HALF AN HOUR LATER, Sabina was sitting at a small dining room table, a towel wrapped around her, shoulder exposed. Thomas was behind, carefully cleaning her wound, dabbing up the blood with cotton wool from her small first aid kit. She bit her lip. It was quite painful. In this position, Thomas could see a birthmark on the back of Sabina's left shoulder—four intersecting lines—two black and two red. It looked like two crosses, one inverted, overlapping each other. *Quite extraordinary*, he thought. *Can it be a coincidence? To be rescued by a woman bearing the mark of the cross while robbing the holy grave?*

Thomas leaned in closer as he continued dabbing; he could see it was a real birthmark, not a tattoo.

"Looking at my birthmark?" Sabina asked, inspecting the room.

"Ah, yes. I thought it might be a tat."

"No. I know what you mean, though. My ex-husband insisted that I must have gotten the red lines tattooed to compliment the black, even when my mother told him otherwise."

"I can see why he's your ex." As he spoke, Thomas snuck out his phone, and with a few taps, set up to take a photo of Sabina's birthmark. He talked a little bit louder, touching Sabina's back here and there, trying to hide his excitement. "Okay, here's the tough part. I need to put in two stitches. It'll only take a moment."

He came around in front of Sabina, giving her cheek a funny squeeze.

"My mysterious lady, bite on this if the pain gets to be too much." He handed Sabina a rolled-up hand towel.

Sabina held the wad of cloth between her teeth, feeling foolish. She winced as Thomas dabbed the area with alcohol. He carefully applied the first stitch, more expertly than first-aid training would explain. Pain spread through Sabina's shoulder. She bit hard on the towel, suddenly glad to have it.

Thomas smoothed a thick plaster over the wound. "Check-mate! Look! All done! You did well, girl. That's a waterproof plaster, by the way..."

Sabina got up, feeling unsteady. He helped her to the bath-room. The walls were tiled in green earth tones with several hanging plants beautifying the space. The color made Sabina happy. It seemed all the negative energy leaped away. The One who created her had helped again. She looked at her reflection in the mirror, whispering, "It will guard you as a mother does her little child."

Thomas waited until he heard running water. He quickly took off his jacket and untucked a dull, flat plate of dirty metal that was stuck in his beltline. He examined it, poured the kettle over it, bit-by-bit, while wiping it with the bloody hand towel. It was a thin bronze tablet, black with age, stamped with a dense Hebrew script. Thomas put it down on the sheets, taking a photo. Satisfied with the result, he wrote a short message to his patron, attaching the picture of the script and Sabina's birthmark.

Sabina finished drying her hair. It dawned on her that not only had she no clothes in the bathroom, but they were also, in fact, in the boot of Holmes, parked securely in an old wooden garage, behind the two-story B&B cottage they were staying in. *I'm sure Thomas won't mind seeing me naked*, she thought to herself. Wrapped in a fresh towel, she stepped out of the bathroom. The heater was on, housed in an older stone fireplace. Thomas was sitting on the bedquilt, shoes off, top button undone, looking at his phone. Sabina sat on the other side of the bed, picked up her phone, pretending to flip through emails.

"A penny for your thoughts?" said Thomas, studying her face.

"Mmm...the bathroom, it's beautiful," Sabina said the first thing that came to mind. She felt nervous but at the same time safe.

"I guess it is." Thomas didn't look away from her face. He stepped closer and lifted his hands to gently cradle her upper arms, skin on skin. "I want to thank you for saving my life, Sabina. I didn't know I was dragging you into trouble. I'm eternally grateful that you saved me."

Sabina didn't know what to say. She felt a warmth towards this man welling up inside her, pride in having helped him, a growing curiosity about the whole situation–why the gunman was there at all?

Thomas gently touched her towel. "I'm sorry. I shouldn't touch you."

"You can touch me." Immediately after saying the words, which had come to her lips like the most natural thing in the world, Sabina's face flushed with heat. *Oh my god, Sabina! You can't say touch me. You just met!*

Thomas looked surprised but returned his hands...this time to her waist. They stood near the bed, taking in each other's faces. Sabina blushed, but she was too connected to the moment to shy away. Their eyes locked. Sabina moved her face a little closer to his. Thomas shivered in anticipation, causing Sabina to smile. *At least he's feeling what I am...*

They kissed. Sabina thought it would be awkward or coltish. Instead, it was hungry and exhilarated. She felt a strange connection with Thomas, something she hadn't experienced in a long time.

Sabina pushed Thomas towards the bed. When he lay back, she climbed on top to kiss him again. She started unbuttoning his shirt, wanting to feel his skin on hers. Rather than helping, Thomas caressed her shape through the towel, then explored under it, sliding a hand up, to stroke the contour of her hip. Sabina pulled Thomas's shirt open, looking down with triumph: she could see the lay of each muscle on his stomach. She let out a squeal of lust, running her hands down his body– lower and lower.

An hour later, Thomas and Sabina lay entangled under the sheets. Sabina let his warmth soak into her, enjoying the simple pleasure of being held with affection. Her shoulder hurt less than she thought it would. Being with Thomas stood out in stark contrast to her experiences with Dario. The way he had caressed her hair, rather than gripping her head. How gentle he had been...How he had given her control...

"Are you alright?" Thomas said softly.

Sabina nodded.

"I don't feel safe here in Bingerbruck. We can't go back to the site, at least until it's set up properly, with increased security. What I'm trying to say... I'm planning to fly to Istanbul, to visit the Hagia Sophia." Thomas watched her face. "I booked while you were showering. There's a flight that leaves today, early morning."

All of a sudden, Sabina felt sad and abandoned. Her mind agreed, it wasn't safe here, but her heart didn't want him to go.

"I booked two tickets, Sabina. Please, come with me to ancient Constantinople. I promise we'll come back to Germany when it's free from danger."

She got the feeling of being manipulated. Why on earth would someone invite her to Istanbul? Her... unseen, unknown, invisible, a woman, who had been dependent on her husband and family almost her whole life, a woman of passive power and fearful dreams about human pleasures. How strange it was!

CHAPTER 5

LEAP OF FAITH

SABINA WAS TIRED. She wouldn't admit it—her Sicilian blood and difficult marriage had taught her to keep her mouth shut. She was also worried about leaving her beloved old Holmes alone. Thomas reassured her that they could store the car in a long-term lock-up near the airport. However, once she had made the decision, Sabina felt excited. She had never been to Turkey. Dario hated traveling; even their honeymoon was spent in Italy. She felt anxious about the flight, but still very grateful that Thomas took her as his trusted company.

In her fantasy, Istanbul was the greatest mark of fallen empires: Roman, Byzantine, and Ottoman. It was neither Asian nor European–a unique place with a vibrant culture, cuisine, and history. She checked a couple of websites and realized she would love to travel, to see the world, to take pictures. She never could... and now she had a chance!

The Majestic Hagia Sophia, one of the largest cathedrals in the world, was on Sabina's "Top Three Things to do in Istanbul" list. It was built in the sixth century by the Byzantine Emperor

Justinian I and later converted into an imperial mosque by Sultan Mehmed II. The history of the cathedral fascinated Sabina. She knew the trip was meant to be. She made the right choice by escaping Palermo and following the lead of Nazarene. The other two things on the top-three list were: warm salep and exploring the Grand Bazaar, a real shopping heaven. She planned to buy spices and herbs for her mother, a leather belt for her father, and the bottle of raki (anise-flavoured vodka) for Matteo.

Thomas interrupted her dreams by telling it was time for breakfast. He'd made cheese and ham sandwiches at the round table with a chequered cloth. They ate in silence, smiling, surrounded by the walls designed seventy years earlier.

"Tell me more about yourself," said Sabina.

"Let me warn you. It's boring. My full name is Thomas von Essen, as you already know. I'm an archaeologist. I like to travel, so if a job includes remote locations, I tend to jump at it."

"Mr. von Essen... is it Dutch?"

"It's a Baltic-German and Swedish noble family, traceable back to the early sixteen-hundreds. My grandfather worked as a military governor in Finland, where he was seriously injured. On the way back home, on the boat, he met Magdalene Elizabeth Brach. She was an American actress, a beginner only, but very passionate about acting. They fell in love and married. The rest, as they say, is history. It's quite extraordinary to find love at the moment you feel like everything is falling apart. Don't you think?"

"Ah, I'd love to know more!" Sabina winked, "I'm afraid I'm a Ferrara, which means 'one who lived by a forge.' Basically, I'm a Smith. Not that special at all. We shall have to keep our romance a deadly secret, Mister von Essen!"

Thomas broke out in a broad grin at the mention of romance.

"I don't know. I'm the black sheep of the family anyway. I'd say, let the world know and damn the consequences!"

"Are you really the black sheep of your family?"

Thomas made a so-so gesture with his hand.

"I miss a lot of official gatherings and tend to post my gifts to nieces, rather than delivering them by myself."

"Hmm. My brother is like that," Sabina frowned. "But he doesn't have your excuses. He lives in the same city."

"Life has a way of complicating things..."

Thomas tried to avoid conversation about romance or the von Essen family. He kissed Sabina, overpowering her doubts. He believed that women loved a dark twist mixed with a humble light. That's why as soon as he got the chance, he jumped to the tale about his archaeological work in the caves of Gargas, near Montrejeau (French Pyrenees). It was a well-prepared lie. Thomas had never been to Gargas: he truly disliked dirty caves, grottos, shelters, and darkness.

He told Sabina that Gargas had its own Jack the Ripper (around 1780), who used the caves as his refuge. Thomas often told that juicy story to the women he slept with or wanted to impress.

"Real Ripper?" Sabina looked curious.

"Yeah, if I remember well, his name was Blaise Ferrage. He cut off the breasts and thighs of his victims, pulled out their intestines and liver, which he ate afterward. The local newspapers reported that he killed over eighty victims until he was arrested and executed. Just imagine, I worked in that legendary cave!"

"Legendary?" Sabina was shocked.

She wasn't sure anymore if following Thomas to Istanbul

was the right decision. He was too reckless, too intense, too cynical. His life seemed like the epitome of *Mr. Cool* from a foreign movie. Even though they were very different, like an apple and a snake, she couldn't let him go—the sex was too good. Or maybe it was only the hunger? The hunger for love and affection?

Sabina and Thomas drove to Frankfurt airport. The first half of the journey was patches of suburbia and neat, densely cultivated farms. Some of the homesteads looked like they were out of a fairy tale. They had crossed a broad bridge over the Rhein, seen the plunging into the Mönchbruch von Mörfelden Nature Reserve, which surrounded the massive airport on all sides. The fifteen-minute drive through winter woodlands thriving with pine, spruce, and beechwood helped settle Sabina's nervous mood. All that time, she listened to Thomas, kept a smile on her face and maintained attention. His eternal lambada of energy and charm blinded her. She wanted more of him.

"My father always told me, 'think big, act fast, take extra!' This motto will work better than any American dream, Baby. I'm so excited you are following! I feel this journey is our path to happiness. What do you think?" Thomas added, checking his phone. He expected a message from his 'dolls,' a team of four, which he carefully picked for dangerous job in Istanbul.

Sabina was silent. She thought about her own father. Frank told her once that a truly good man has no desire to be known or admired by others. A good man should be himself, only then he is completely with God. *One more junk hero?* Sabina thought while watching how Thomas drove to a twenty-four-hour garage facility. He paid at the electronic pillbox by credit card and drove Holmes inside his future secure home. Sabina placed a hand on the bonnet, affectionately rubbing the purple paintwork. "I'll come back and get you, my boy. I won't be long, Holmes, dear..."

They loaded Sabina's bags into a taxi and rode out to the airport, watching how the snow, once again, began its heavy fall.

"Oh! I hope this doesn't delay our flight," Sabina said anxiously.

The old taxi driver answered, with a thick German accent, "Don't worry. There will be no delay. Our planes don't care about this." The driver gestured at the road.

The airport was gigantic. Flurries of snow glowed in the air, illuminated by dozens of floodlights that lit up the tracks and forecourts. Snowplows cleared the roads and runways. Thousands of people streamed in and out of its entrances. Inside, surrounded by luggage carts, businesspeople, and families with kids, they shed their coats. Sabina wore a tight black dress with a ruffled skirt she had always felt pretty in. Thomas found the appropriate counter for the luggage and stood in line to have their passports stamped. When Sabina turned away from the desk, tucking her passport back into the handbag, she noticed a strange figure across the room full of travellers. The man was dressed in a grey leather coat, average height, and lean. He stood gazing at her. His long face marred by an odd scar. It creased his flesh from the corner of his right eye straight down to his neck. His left eye had been covered with a black patch. Sabina looked at him again. She had never seen him before. A cold feeling in her gut told her that he was the gunman from the grave. She glanced away, but it was too late; he had read her as she had read him. The heat drained from her veins. The man stood in the same spot, unmoved. Sabina wanted to grab Thomas, but he was still chatting in German with the pretty blonde clerk. Panic started to rise, quickening her breathing.

"What's wrong, dear?" Thomas said, gently taking her arm.

"That man...don't look! The one across the room, with a scar and a black eye patch, in the grey leather jacket. I think it's him! The killer!" Sabina was trembling with fear and anger; she hated being hunted. Thomas firmly steered his lady toward their flight lounge.

"Let's just sit down, okay?"

"No. We should run, Tom. What if he gets on the plane?"

Thomas stopped and said, "Sabina, I understand how you're feeling. In a way, you're right, but it's what he wants us to do...to run. If that man is an assassin, a cold-blooded killer, and for whatever reason, he wants *me* dead...then I'll be dead. I'm so sorry you ended up inside of all that mess." He paused. "I know people like him. He wants us to isolate ourselves, hide in the shithole. What he doesn't want us to do is to stay completely visible and catch our flight."

Sabina was tired of being told what she should believe or do by men. On the other hand, Thomas might be right. She nodded.

After walking through x-ray machines, they stepped inside of the lounge. The room was spacious, with no other ways in or out—safe, with a few locked staff-only doors. Through the glass frontage, Sabina could see their massive Boeing 73888.

They sat in silence, watching the entrance. Sabina was tense, her mind racing. She whispered to Thomas, "Why would he want to kill you? Because of the grave?"

"I don't think so. He was already waiting at the tree and took an opportunity when the snow blew up. I think he has been hired by some enemy of my patron. I have no idea who it could be."

"Why'd you do it? Why'd you dig like that, inside of the grave?" Sabina gripped Tom's arm as she looked nervously around at the travellers and flight staff. Most of them were distracted by their phones, newspapers, or each other.

Thomas sighed. He knew he couldn't avoid this conversation. "When Kushner-Parzinger's team surveyed the sight with sonic imaging, they found the tombstone that led to a different burial space. I was trying to get there before them, to take some photos inside. If you hadn't been by my side, I'd be dead. You are my guardian angel!"

Sabina smiled, trying to alleviate some of the tension gripping her. She elbowed him, whispering, "Don't forget about it. You owe me one!"

A German voice thundered out over the speakers.

"That's us," said Thomas. "We are safe."

Sabina practically ran to the flight checkpoint, with their two tickets in hand. The man in a grey jacket appeared near the chairs. He was explaining something to the tall woman with a manager's badge.

"Oh, God! That's him! Our Ripper! Don't you see it now? He's planning to kill us during the flight!" Sabina's face was filled with fury. "Maybe he's got a team of killers waiting at the other end?"

She started to shake, grabbed the Bible from her handbag and frantically flipped pages. The book was wrapped in soft leather, shabby and old at the corners. Thomas squeezed Sabina's arm, trying to prevent the attention she caused.

"Shhhh. Relax. We'll keep that in mind when we get there, okay? I've arranged a quick getaway for us. I have a team of kick-ass professionals!"

The air hostess smiled at them both as they passed through the doors, "Welcome to Dizzy Clouds Express Airlines!"

Sabina had watched the entrance to the plane until the air hostess secured it. The killer had not boarded the flight. She allowed herself to relax a little, watching the snowfall past the window by her seat. The plane slowly trucked onto the runway. Thomas had his eyes closed, taking slow, deliberate breaths. He lay worrying about what might be waiting for them at the airport in Istanbul, but soon, the weariness of the day suffocated all his fears. He drifted off into a restless sleep. Sabina covered her legs with the blanket, asked for a glass of red wine, preparing to read Psalm 68:

May God arise,
may his enemies be scattered;
may his foes flee before him.
As smoke is blown away by the wind,
may you blow them away.
as wax melts before the fire,
May the wicked perish before God.

She reread it seventeen times, like an obsessive maniac, genuinely enjoying the images arising in her mind. She closed her eyes, placed the head on Thomas's shoulder, and melted away from the warm seat of the plane into the world of wild adventure.

CHAPTER 6

FOUR FRIENDS OR FOUR ENEMIES

NINA CLOSED THE DOOR BEHIND HER AND TOOK IN THE LUXURIOUS HOTEL ROOM. SHE WAS THE LAST. THE TEAM WAS ALREADY HERE, WAITING. NINA WAS SHORT, DARK-HAIRED, SOLID, AND DRESSED IN BLACK TIGHTS, BOOTS, WINDBREAKER, AND CAP. SHE WAS RUSSIAN.

Nina: Lifen, why this meeting? What's going on?

Lifen: *(took a draw on her gold e-cigarette)* It looks like Thomas has got himself into a bit of trouble and has some baggage. He's flying in right now. ETA is three hours and fifteen minutes. He thinks there might be hitmen waiting for him at this end. He wants us to take care of that before he touches down.

LIFEN LOOKED AS IF SHE'D JUST BEEN DRAGGED OUT OF A COCKTAIL PARTY. SHE WORE LOUIS VUITTON HEELS, A LITTLE RED DRESS FROM ARMANI, A BLACK FAUX FUR COAT, AND EMERALD EARRINGS WHICH MATCHED HER MINT GREEN CONTACT LENSES. SHE WAS JURAS-

SIC, WITH BOTH HER APPEARANCE AND ACCENT HARD TO PIN DOWN.

Madison: What. The. Fuck? This is way earlier than we should be having trouble.

Nina: I can understand Interpol being after him, but why does he think hitmen might be waiting at the airport?

Odette: *(chuckled, with the tilt of a French accent)* What is the baggage?

ODETTE LENT ON THE BENCH OF THE MARBLE BUILT-IN KITCHENETTE, WITH FRESH ESPRESSO IN HAND. SHE WAS AN ATTRACTIVE, SLIM BRUNETTE WITH SHORT CURLY HAIR. HER CLOTHES CHOSEN TO ACCENTUATE HER FIGURE.

Lifen: *(enjoying the effect of her words)* He got jumped in a snow flurry by a gunman. A civilian saved him. Now our sweet king von Essen is dragging her here. He said he has good reasons...This gunman might have been at the airport when they fled. Thomas thinks they might have arranged a hit or ambush at this end.

Madison: *(rose up, irritated)* This is fucked. I don't know about the rest of you, but I have no idea. First, who is that HER? And second, who tried to kill Thomas?

MADISON HAD AN OBVIOUS AMERICAN ACCENT. SHE WAS THE TALLEST OF THEM ALL, A BOTTLE BLONDE, FIT FROM TRAINING, BUILT ALMOST LIKE A SOLDIER, WEARING JEANS AND A BROWN LEATHER JACKET.

Lifen: Chill, Mad, it seems pretty transparent. Thomas was hired and set in motion by Papa Zen. We were, in turn, hired by Thomas. No one else knew Thomas's purpose at the dig.

Nina: *(frowned)* You're not trying to say that Papa Zen, the one who's paying our freakin' bills, want to kill us. 'Cause I don't buy it!

Lifen: Maybe not, but my guts are saying it comes from him. Someone in his circle has leaked the information. Or one of his enemies is trying to stop him?

Nina: *(with sarcasm)* Okay, whatever. We need to figure out how to get Mr. von Essen out of the pickle he's in.

Odette: *(moving in circles, touching furniture)* Girls, the way I see it is this...we have a real problem. We have no idea who the assassins are. They could come from any number of gangs, crime families, or even freelances. It's the worst! Plus, we don't know what contacts this possible enemy of Papa Zen has. And the most awful, we don't have any useful contacts in Istanbul ourselves. I'm starting to hate this job, and I haven't started yet!

Madison: She's more than right, the airport is one of the biggest in the world. It's filled with innocent travellers. We can't look for new people in town or suspiciously parked cars. The place is fucking massive; it would take us weeks!!

Lifen: Well, there's only one course we can take. Our potential enemies don't have much time to prepare a perfect operation here. They don't know if Thomas is going to take the taxi or hire a car. This means they're going to have to wait as the flight disembarks, recognize him, shadow him...and then kill. It won't be easy because we'll be there watching them too!

Nina: I agree, but when and where exactly are they planning to hit them? That's the question! We need to save von Essen's dick for future generations.

Lifen: Sha, girl! They can strike at the airport, but it's very crowded. Probably, on the road or at the hotel? I think we need to get rid of them while the wheels are turning. Let's make

Tom and his Hot Squeeze disappear like a mystery wrapped in an enigma.

Madison: *(laughed, nervously)* You know I like a good fight, especially if it is so crazy!

Lifen: I forgot a crucial detail! Tom said he doesn't want the girl to know much. That means, we're meant to pull this off without her knowing we did it.

Madison: *(shouted from the sofa)* Mission Fuckin' Impossible! I'm not kidding!

Nina: *(smiled while pouring vodka at the bar section)* If Tom Cruise can do it, we can do it, too! Just imagine you are in the movies. Cheers!

Lifen: Enough! Listen up! This plan relies on us being separated all the time. We'll keep linked by our earpieces as usual. We'll have two cars circling, Nina and Madison. Odette and I will go in and try to get eyes on who follows Thomas and his Sweet Cake.

LIFEN NODDED TO ODETTE, WHO RETURNED A CONFIDENT SMILE.

Nina: *(on the way to the door)* These men will have guns. We have to keep the firearms in the cars. I'm heading off to fix that right now. See ya!

SHE QUIETLY STEPPED IN INTO THE BRIGHT HALL OF THE FER HOTEL.

Lifen: *(checked her elegant Paul Hewitt watch)* Okay, let's do it. Thomas and his mysterious civilian will touch down at 12:50 pm. We need to be in place by noon, the latest.

TWO BIZARRE SILHOUETTES WALKED OUT OF THE FER HOTEL. THEY DIVIDED INTO TWO DIFFERENT CARS AND DROVE INTO THE SUNRISE.

CHAPTER 7

MISSION IMPOSSIBLE

LIFEN, Madison, Odette, and Nina activated their earpieces. They were linked to their smartphones which formed a peer-to-peer encrypted network through a dongle. After a quick sound off, each confirmed they were in their position.

The Istanbul Airport was tremendous: it sat thirty-five kilometers north-west of the center, brightly lit, bustling with the population of a small city. Nina and Madison circled through the interconnected roadways, which swept into the airport, then off to the surrounding towns. Nina was in a deep blue Fiat 500C Star model, a compact and standard car. Madison drove a large grey Jeep with tinted windows. She loved everything big and suspicious. Lifen, still dressed for a cocktail party, but with dark sunglasses on, waited near the debarking lounge where Thomas's flight was supposed to dock in a few minutes. The space around bustled with travellers hauling baggage, studded in shops, lounges, cafes, and service desks. Near the shelter of a white pillar, amidst all the chaos, stood Odette. She was holding a hand-drawn sign "Welcome to Our Honeymoon!" written in French.

Lifen had texted the plan to Thomas's phone yesterday. She received a reply only when he landed: I have little choice but to stick to your plan. I'll be a good boy.

She smiled when she read it. Two minutes later, passengers began walking through the archway, into the common hall. Lifen could see Thomas holding the hand of an attractive woman with dark wavy hair, in her mid-thirties. *If he's dragged her to Istanbul because she's a good lay, I'll castrate him*, Lifen thought as she watched them passing by. She followed them about ten meters back. Thomas wore a grey backpack. He looked tired but was smiling and talking to the woman by his side. The woman pulled a huge travel bag. Anyone could tell that she was exceptional: strength, resilience, and hope shined through her face.

Odette's voice came over the earpiece, "I'm twenty meters behind you, Lin. Check—a cute boy, sharp suit, thick neck. He is following the mark. You should peel off, Sweetie, before he realizes who you are."

"He's all yours, I'll get ice cream." Lifen diverted to an ice cream stand. She started eyeing their spellbinding selection of Gelato. "What do you think, girls? Does food eaten on missions contain calories?"

"I think," came Nina's humorless voice, "you shouldn't think about calories when Thomas is here. Greatest fucker ever made! You said that, not me."

Lifen laughed. Sometimes she loved the dirty side of Nina's humor.

Odette shadowed the young man. He was thickset Eurotrash with his neat hair buzzed almost bald on the back and sides. Thomas stopped at a kiosk. He bought two take-away coffees.

The young man passed him, pretending to look through a selection of posters outside a news agency. Odette stopped near the news, too. She bought a magazine and took a couple of selfies with the shops in the background. She said to the others, "They got coffee. Thomas is making a call, probably checking the hire car. Ready to go."

"I'll wait till I see them," replied Nina. "I'm going to circle ahead to the hire car platform. Jump in Madison's car, Oddie. I'll be on the road soon. I can't pick you up."

"Where's bad boy's car?" asked Madison. "I mean, if they parked in the car park, they'd never catch us unless they put a tracer on Thomas's hire."

"I passed them," Nina's responded. "There's a car pulled up on the side of the drive-through with hazard lights on, near the exit for hire deport. One guy at the wheel, another is checking under the bonnet. Who are they? Why do they look so perfect...young, dumb, and full of cum?!?"

"Good job, Nina," said Lifen with coldness in her voice. She was happy that their plan was falling into place. "In that case, Odette and I are heading to the front to get picked up. We'll take this fight out to the road."

On the way to the car, Lifen texted Thomas, asking to share his live location with Madison or Nina through the JungleBumpRoad app. It would help them find him without any effort.

Odette and Lifen hurried to the front doors of the airport, into the sizeable no-parking pickup area, which was filled with cars loading and unloading their boots, people hugging hellos and kissing goodbyes. They could see it was raining outside. Nina pulled up in the Fiat, picking up Lifen. After a couple of minutes, a grey Jeep picked up Odette, who wrinkled her nose at the dull interior of the car.

"Why did you get this ugly thing?" Odette asked mystified. "You could have gotten a cool car on our budget!"

Madison grinned. "I like a car that can take a bit of punishment. You know what I mean?"

"They are for driving, not punishing! This one is absolutely uncomfy."

Madison rolled her eyes as she pulled away; she began driving the long loop, the comeback around past the hire car exit.

"Are all of you cheese-eating surrender monkeys so negative?" Madison glanced at Odette.

The French beauty said something in her native language–indeed an insult; though what exactly it was, Madison could only guess. After a minute of silence, Odette added, "At least my country isn't ruled by a pumpkin in a toupee!"

Madison laughed. She pulled out her phone, stuck it to a pad on the dash, checking the tracking link to Thomas. She could see he was already on the road, looping around to leave the airport.

"How close to bad boys are you, Nina?" asked Madison, concerned.

"Catching up. I'll be close enough when they reach the highway. I saw three in the car. I guess your first boy must have jogged down and jumped in," said a voice in a Russian accent.

Madison increased her speed, taking every opportunity in the dense traffic to move ahead. When she got to the highway, she could finally see Thomas—her car was about four-hundred meters behind. Madison started slowly closing the gap. Nina was speeding southeast toward Istanbul on a three-lane highway, separated from opposing traffic by a low cement barrier. It was hard to see through a wash of grey rain, but she didn't give up. She was almost there...

A larger blue sedan followed Thomas's small black hire car. Nina noticed how one of the men lifted a large handgun. The rain fragmented the image on the windows, but she was sure—he was preparing to kill.

Nina said to Lifen, "I spotted one of the assassins in the back seat. It seems he is checking a submachine gun. They're not going to let Thomas get to the hotel. We need to stop them. NOW!"

"A firefight? In the rain? On the highway? Oh, I just bought a new dress. Does anyone have a smart plan?" asked Lifen.

"Fuck yeah, I do!" shouted Madison. "It's got to be short and sharp—listen carefully..." Madison detailed her plan in the bluntest terms. The others listened in stunned silence. "Mmm, a good plan," said Nina. "Should be no problem."

"What? The plan is crazy! There has to be a better way," said Odette.

"There's no time to discuss," decided Lifen. "Your plan is good to go, Mad."

She took out her phone and called Thomas. "There's a massive truck yard about one click ahead of you on the right. Go in there. It's a dead-end but has lots of space. If they follow you in, come out, and continue driving. If they don't, stay there."

The truck yard was prominent—a sweeping road that went into a cluttered space defined by semi-permanent cement barriers and rammed earth. Nina saw the small black hire car turn off. She slowed near the cement barrier and pulled over. The grey Jeep passed by and stopped as well. The assassin's car slowed near the entrance, then quickly turned into the yard and out of sight.

"Perfect. Next move...get out and jump in the car behind us," Madison grinned.

Odette was visibly upset. "This is a stupid plan, let's do something else!"

"No time! Look, I've got years of practice doing smash-em-up-derby! I'll be fine."

"What even is that?"

"Get your ass out, Oddie!" Madison pushed Odette out of the seat.

Odette slammed the door. She hurried back through the cold rain to the blue Fiat. She climbed into the back, shacking. Inside, she found Lifen—full of tension and Nina—calm, eating an apple.

"Why are you eating a fucking apple?" whispered Odette.

"It cleans my teeth."

"What if Madison dies? Do you have any feelings at all? She's going to die!" yelled Odette.

"What are you, lovers? She will be fine," said Nina. "Madison is too stupid to die."

CHAPTER 8

ACCIDENTAL DEATH

MADISON WATCHED Thomas's position on the small glowing screen of her phone. As soon as she saw the indicator heading out of the truck yard, she pulled up onto the highway and started accelerating. She saw Thomas's car speed out of the merging road without a pause because of the sedan behind it. Madison gripped the wheel tight. Now or never!

The sedan drew up to a pause, waiting for a truck to pass. Madison let out a whoop *winning*, punching the accelerator swerved off the road and straight at the side of the assassin's car. Adrenalin hit Madison's head like a hammer—the world slowed down. For a moment, she could see each raindrop falling above her; she could see the dumbstruck faces of the men in the car, eyes wide, like scared animals, struggling with the blazing light of her headlamps.

The cars impacted, making a horrible cacophony. The sedan folded partly in half and was sent tumbling two car lengths. The men inside, engulfed in a hell of screaming, broken glass, and blood. The airbag opened and absorbed Madison's body. At first, she snapped forward, then tossed back in her seat. She was too high, too excited. Madison stabbed the airbag and stepped out of the car. She felt like floating, but despite all that dizziness, she pulled out a shotgun that sat in a leather holster, a sawn-off semiautomatic, stock cut back to a pistol grip.

Madison walked to the car, enjoying how steam poured from under its bonnet. It was lying on its side, engine towards her. Hearing breaking glass, she jogged up and whirled around, facing the front window. On the highway, passers-by gawked—fleeting shocked faces behind rainswept glass.

Odette screamed when the cars collided, the Jeep's bonnet buckling. Nina indicated to merge and started rapidly approaching the scene. Madison watched how a man had pushed out the shattered windscreen and crawled out. He was covered in blood. He noticed female boots and shoved back onto his haunches and brought the gun up to bare, eyes wild, face puffy, and smashed. Madison unloaded her shotgun with a smile, one-handed. The assassin's elbow exploded in gore. His lower arm, still holding the sub, fell on the muddy ground. The man lifted the mangled stump, staring at it in dawning horror. Madison was already on top of him. She stabbed her punch-dagger into his throat. It wasn't enough... She added five more punches into his chest before he collapsed. Crouching, she looked into the car's cabin—both men were unconscious—the one in the rear mangled, almost split open where the car had caved in and sheared into his body. Madison coldly levelled her shotgun on the front passenger. With a thunderous bang, she reduced his head to a bowl of brains. In this exact moment, the Fiat pulled up, an astonished Odette stared out the window at the dead men.

"Good work!" said Lifen, opening the window. "Do you feel up to the driving, mad girl?"

"Ha! Sure, I'm fine," answered Madison. It was the best day of her life.

"How can she be fine? No, no, no! She just had a crash! She shouldn't drive, please!" Odette pleaded.

"Shut up! Lifen said. "Go check the boys, and do not forget to clean up."

Odette whispered something in French, tired and demolished to bits. She dreamed of taking a bath with Tranquil Isle salt and a gentle massage. If only he'd reply to her messages today, but it seems, Thomas had been too busy tasting his new Sicilian fruit. Odette hated her. That woman was the reason they had drifted apart again.

About a year ago, Odette was diagnosed with love-obsessive behavior and erotomania. She was fixated on Thomas and their delusional relationships. Thomas invited Odette to the group because he was terrified of her sickness. He also believed it would be easier to control the illness if he'd be able to keep her close by. The stalking behavior had disappeared, but the jealousy increased in proportions.

Madison climbed in her Jeep and turned the key. It rumbled to life, one of the headlamps even worked. Madison grinned in triumph. She did it! She saved her lover from death. She leaned back in her seat, relaxing after stressful events, waiting for the command to leave.

Lifen looked back at still-shocked Odette. "Touching anything in that car without gloves is a forensic nightmare. I'd rather not, but if you think there's something that could help us find who sent these pricks, then maybe it's worth it—do it fast."

Odette swallowed and went out of the blue car. She stared

over at the body sprawled sideways in the mud, the casual suit, middle-aged, northern European. He's not local and probably not gang-related; they've got to be assets put in place by some organization with clout, or maybe here by dumb luck.

"Time is ticking, chicken! What do you see?" Lifen gave the French beauty a small ironic smile. Sometimes things were just too funny.

"Nothing. They've got nothing of use," stammered Odette, wet and cold.

"That's what I guessed, too. Have you heard it, Nina?" Lifen asked, pushing her hair back.

"Many of those who sleep in the dust of the earth shall awake. Some to everlasting life. Some to shame. Some to die again," Nina announced through the open window.

"She scares me. Is she serious?" Odette shivered.

"That's what Russians are for... to scare," answered Lifen, while trying to call Thomas. He didn't answer. She wanted to spend this night with him, on the big bed with the cherrywood headboard, surrounded by gold antique lamps. She wanted appreciation for organizing the whole operation to save dumb von Essen's ass. She dreamed about rough sex on the carpet, followed by an ache in her knees from the night of love. She wanted to feel numb from the excitement of their passion. She simply couldn't stop thinking about him. She wanted to be the one.

Lifen flipped through old messages, sighed, and commanded to leave the place. Two cars pulled onto the highway. Soon, the scene of carnage vanished behind them. After gathering herself, Lifen sent a single text: Laundry's done.

. . .

Sabina was feeling better. When the plane landed, she had been immediately plunged into bright lights and fresh coffee inside the splendid sprawl of the Istanbul airport. She was fascinated by Flow Rooms—white walls in different shapes, that ran through 19,000 square meters of space. The structure and groove of Istanbul were too dynamic. She didn't expect that from the capital of her dreams, ancient Constantinople. The vibe of the place broke all traditional boundaries.

At first, she had been disoriented and frightened, looking everywhere for imagined killers, but of course, finding none. In the hire car, she was momentarily distracted by the style of the architecture around her. It was modern, with clean-cut lines and the original facades mixed in with multipurpose buildings. She focused on prayer and maintaining a religious peace of mind, forgetting about her partner. They drove in silence, lonely highways drenched in the rain. Thomas began receiving text messages, which seemed to agitate him.

"Is everything okay, Thomas?" asked Sabina.

"More or less. We're having a bit of trouble with the hotel." He looked apologetic. "Hopefully, it'll sort out soon."

Further down the road, he received another text. "I better pull over and make a call, okay? I'll see if I can sort this out. That truck depo might have some space to park."

He turned into a fenced yard, cluttered with demountable buildings, dozens of trucks, and clusters of grimy men, drinking coffee under canvas awnings. Sabina could see headlights blurring through the rain: another car had followed them in.

"Actually," said Thomas all of a sudden, "I don't think we're meant to be in here. Hmmm, it might be a building site or something." He looped around through muddy tracks and drove back out the same road.

At the highway, Thomas merged recklessly and sped toward Istanbul. Sabina looked back. She noticed the lights of a car rotating on a circular axis. It left shines and sparkles across the highway.

"I can't believe it. I think a car just had an accident behind us," she said, surprised.

"Really? Behind us? Don't worry. They're close to that truck stop and the main road from the airport. I'd say they'll have an ambulance with them in no time, dear. No point stopping and calling it in. I'm sure there are plenty of witnesses there."

Sabina nodded. A minute later, Thomas got another text. He smiled, looking genuinely relieved.

"It's all good now. We've got the room. The management of the hotel apologizes for the inconvenience."

CHAPTER 9

MR. AND MRS. KNOPF

ISTANBUL WAS a daunting maze during the day. Most of the time, Sabina stared at the people and architecture. The city was famous for its ancient structures, but what she saw were mostly modern buildings, western clothes, and expensive European cars.

The rain had reduced to a drizzle. They drove deeper into the city, closer to the antique heart of Istanbul. There were fewer and fewer people on the streets. Thomas pulled up in front of a luxury hotel made of stone, with elaborate wooden balconies. A Turkish man in a thobe and turban came down, willing to help. Unfolding an umbrella, he opened Sabina's door.

"Shall I escort you inside, ma'am?"

"One minute...I forgot my handbag," said Sabina, twisting around, partly climbing into the back seat to reach her bag. Her dress pulled tight around her hips as she bent over. The Turkish gentleman averted his gaze. Thomas did not. "Here it is. Let's go." Sabina climbed out of the car, following happy Thomas up to the doors of the Sultanahmet Palace HotTel.

The foyer was lined with lacquered wood panelling and had a high plaster ceiling. The doorman held out his hand for the keys and turned to Thomas. "Shall I park your car in our garage and bring the luggage to your room, Sir?"

"That would be very convenient. Thank you." Thomas said, giving him the keys.

At the desk, they were greeted by a neat woman with a blue headscarf.

"We've got a booking for Mr. and Mrs. Knopf," said Thomas, giving Sabina a roguish grin. Sabina stared at him, blushing. A footman led them through the old building, with the corridors wall-papered in odd designs, to a retrofitted elevator.

Inside the room, they found a spacious chamber: the plaster of the walls enhanced with bold paintings, the leather and oak furniture resting on a deep-green carpet overlaid with gold lines. Thomas slumped in a chair. Sabina sauntered over to the double doors leading to the bedroom. She pushed them open, revealing a large king-size bed with a beautiful floral cover, lit by the residual light from the living room.

She turned to Thomas, laughing, "I feel you booked this room before we became lovers!"

Thomas looked over at the bed innocently. "I suppose I did..."

"I think...," Sabina sunk on her knees before his chair, "... that you intended to seduce me here regardless of whether you managed it in Germany."

She leaned into his hips.

"I am rather taken with you..."

"Why is that?" she teased.

"I believe that God sent you. I think you're my guardian angel. I cannot stop thinking of the serendipity of your arrival.

I think God wanted me to live. He wanted my work to succeed. That's why I met you."

"Really?" Sabina paused. "That's not what I thought you were going to say, Thomas. When are you going to tell me more about your job?"

"Soon. Very soon," Thomas smiled, kissing her shoulders.

"Time for a shower. Ladies first!" Sabina rose, pulling off her boots. She quickly checked her phone and escaped to the bathroom. Thomas still sat in a chair, listening to the running water, wondering if he should join her. His lethargy kept him in place. He looked as Sabina padded out of the bathroom, wearing nothing but a bathrobe. She paused, glanced back at Thomas, inviting him into the bedchamber.

Thomas studied the pressed-metal ceiling, thinking about his plans. He rolled a little to check on Sabina. She had held him tightly after their lovemaking, fallen asleep in his arms, just like the last time. The room was still dark, but a single sliver of light had already penetrated through the gap in the curtain, illuminating Sabina's legs, lips, and hair. Thomas got up, started dressing. He had picked her as submissive and naïve, and yes, she certainly was very trusting, but when they made love, she was different: assertive, powerful, dominating. There was a disconnect. The woman he made love to was different from the woman who walked by him during the day. *There is more in you than you ever know,* he thought, touching Sabina's hair.

Thomas picked up an umbrella, let himself out of the bedroom, and walked downstairs to collect the keys. He drove the hire-car across town to a small, abandoned theatre, nestled amidst poor tenements, near the Cathedral of the Holy Apostles. He parked in the gloom of the alley and walked down to the theatre, trying to make out the shape of a side door. He knocked four times. The voice behind the door asked for the password.

"Jesus is here. Fear not," Thomas said.

CHAPTER 10

CONSPIRACY

A TINY FEMALE FIGURE, a piece of black in the dark, opened the door. Thomas followed her. They walked down a dusty corridor, guided by pale light creeping around the edges. The small woman opened the gate to a lit room beyond, light enveloping her. She was short, dressed in leather—her ghostly face hemmed in funny locks.

"Hey, Nina," said Thomas as he passed her. Of the four women Thomas had hired, Nina was the only one he did not want to sleep with. It was not that she wasn't attractive (in her way, she was sweet and special), but he disliked her cold eyes, unsmiling lips, and weird sense of humor. Not that it mattered in the bed, though.

Yes, of course, Thomas always tried to maintain a strictly professional relationship, but with the other three beauties, it was rather painful to keep his hands away. He remembered how he got himself into big trouble when he met Lifen in Singapore. After a one-night stand, Lifen decided that they were meant to be. She believed that some kind of karmic process had been involved in their sexual games. At first,

Thomas tried to say "no," but Lifen explained that she is a part of the Yakuza family (or at least her tattoo), and it's hazardous to decline Yakuza. She also had exceptional loving skills—she could torture Thomas for hours with an admiring attitude, shamanic passion, and enormous imagination. He would never push away a girl with such expertise; his ego needed her.

The room was gross. A collapsed stage with trick doors and platforms, revealed in its ruin, sat at one end of the hall; scaffolding dominated the ceiling with arrays of dead lights pointing here and there. It was filled with inexplicable junk: mannequins, ruined tables, old sofas, bolts of cloth, piles of magazines, and broken bottles. Amidst all this, a circle of dilapidated armchairs surrounded a low table; one corner was held up by a soapbox, on which sat beer, vodka, scotch, and champagne. Around the table were the other three women: Lifen Ong—the wealthy daughter of famous Korean moneybag, pretending-to-be-Yakuza; Madison Black—the Texan girl, raised by paramilitary doomsday preppers, and Odette Donadieu—the alluring French thief.

Odette embraced him. "Tommy, my luv! You're okay! I am so happy! Come sit down and have a drink. I made sure there was champagne. You wouldn't believe what these girls drink."

Thomas sat, accepting a full sparkling glass from Odette's hands.

"You look terrible, Thomas. If you want, I can help you to get back into the proper mood," Nina said, showing a small line of cocaine on the table.

"No, thanks. I'm a bit jet lagged. I'll be okay."

"Business first," said Lifen, arching a thin dark eyebrow. "Why on earth are we in Istanbul? Our budget is running very low. Soon we'll have to ask Papa Zen for more money…He is not going to like that if we've got nothing for him. Or did we?"

"Don't worry. Everything is going surprisingly well, apart from those assassins hounding our heels," Thomas replied.

Odette laughed nervously. "It was scary! Do you think they're going to be a further problem, because…"

"I don't think they'll have the time to find us," Thomas stopped her.

"Is that just a guess?" asked Madison, pursing her lips. "Why don't you tell us everything we need to know."

"Ladies! Please, shut up! Uncle Thomas is here to help. Let me explain."

Thomas was irritated. All he wanted was to deliver Sabina and whatever they'd find in Istanbul to Papa Zen as soon as possible. He had planned his escape from this madness for almost a week.

"So much P-O-W-E-RRRRR! Go ahead, make me feel better, Uncle Tom!" giggled Odette, gazing at him with call-to-bedroom eyes.

Thomas couldn't stand her drunk flirting. Odette was unstoppable and wild when she was stoned or tipsy. He knew she would try to seduce him today. And he knew he'd never been able to resist. Thomas liked sex with Lifen, but Odette was a healer, some kind of psychopomp of sensual action. Her animal sound, perfect breasts, and French talking made his knees weak.

"Come closer, Uncle," purred Odette, beckoning with a finger. "We can play those special games you like."

"Just so you know," said Madison, "your uncle is full of cum already, after the night with his new *baggage*."

"Stop it! I don't find this cute," Lifen said, and turned an angry face to the table.

"Goodness, we're only having fun," explained Odette, flushing.

"Alright, my ladies. I'll give you the facts and leave you out the fluff," said Thomas. He was getting tired from the empty conversations and stupid chats.

Suddenly, Lifen looked straight at him, and asked, "Is the *fluff* where you got so blue-balled that you picked yourself up a little Italian whore and dragged her halfway around the world?"

Thomas rolled his eyes. "Lin, Darling! Don't start it again! I was at the dig. She was there by chance. An opportunity arose to try to get to the inner grave, so I left that little bitch on the watch. She had no idea what was going on...I got to the gravestones—that's all that matters! A gunman turned up, but we got away. If it weren't for Sabina, I certainly would have died. I swear I was going to vanish in the night and make my way here, but..."

"But *what*?" asked Lifen.

"I noticed a birthmark on her shoulder when I was dressing her bullet wound." Thomas showed the photo on his phone. "I thought it was extraordinary, such a special mark. See, it looks like two crosses together. Add to that—we met by the grave of the Nazarene's family..."

"An interesting birthmark isn't a reason to drag a dumb pussycat into our dangerous game," noted Lifen, drinking scotch.

"Maybe, but that's not what Papa Zen thought. I sent him this photo along with a picture of the bronze tablet I found. He said to keep the Italian girl close. Attention now, Lovelies! He will raise our pay another quarter-of-a-million if we deliver her with the book! Alive!"

"Why? What does that birthmark even mean?" Odette asked, eyes widening.

"I have no idea but seeing as each of you is making an extra fifty-thousand dollars from Sabina's presence, I wouldn't be too harsh on her."

Thomas enjoyed the greed in the eyes of Madison and Odette. He sat near them on the dirty sofa, hugging both girls. Odette bowed and picked up a very old *Psychologies* magazine, sticking out of the crack in the floor. The cover delivered alarming messages: "16 ways to melt his heart," "Mindful sex after marriage," "Fight for the place in his bedroom," "Get ready for love." Odette's obsession with her boss had been known very well. She met him in Paris a couple of years ago, helping to rob a famous jewellery shop. She had followed him ever since.

Where're all the gins and fairies when you need them? Thomas thought, dreaming about the end of his suffering.

"You know," said Nina sipping vodka through a straw, "you are stabbing the chick in the back."

"Am I? Let's not jump to conclusions, Nina. We have no reason to believe Papa Zen has sinister intentions. Or do we?" In moments like this, Thomas always regretted he wasn't a killer.

Nina sneered. "Come on, boss. We're kinda kidnapping her. He might not even care about that tat. What if he likes her pale skin or how her curly hair falls on her shoulders like that?" She imitated the move with her head, grinning. "Papa Zen is a man. Men are evil."

"Enough," said Lifen. "What's done is done. We all want the extra money, so let's not let our morals get in the way. Anyway, that's not what matters. Are we here because of the lost pages of the Bible, Thomas?"

"Yes. Seems, the bronze tablet I dragged out says exactly where it is, or at least, where it was. The place has been changed during the past years, but there's a small chance it's still there. Everything is going according to plan, ladies. Cheers!"

There were smiles all around; drinks were raised.

"Okay," Lifen smiled. "What about the boys we met at the airport?"

Thomas shrugged. "Papa Zen has been informed. I'd say so —let's work quickly and carefully. Hopefully, we'll be on a private jet out of here before they have any clue where we are. Not to mention, there might not be anyone else in the city looking for us right now." Thomas felt happy. He believed in his lucky star.

Sabina drifted up out of the well of dreams. For a moment, she looked at the ornate pattern of interwoven ropes depicted on the pressed metal ceiling. Then the mystery evaporated, and the events of the last two days leapt back to her mind. She sat up. She was alone in the room. And naked. She didn't sleep nude usually, preferring silk pyjamas. The sounds of the city outside beckoned to her senses. A peek out the window showed that it was still raining. Sabina donned a flowing green dress and a scarf. *Hopefully, this dress won't be ruined by a bullet,* she thought, walking downstairs to the restaurant.

She was only one of five people eating breakfast that early in the morning. Sabina admired her full Turkish breakfast: fresh bread, three kinds of cheese, bergamot jam on the side, spicy sausage, and eggs, accompanied by an ornate teapot, wafting with the strong scent of brewing black tea. She was marvelling at the heady aromatic flavour of the jam when

Thomas strolled into the room. He was dressed in a casual grey suit, carrying strange shopping bags.

"Good morning, Sabina, you're looking radiant."

"Flattery. We, women, can't live without it."

"I bought you something." Thomas lifted one of the bags and set it down by her.

Sabina pulled the contents of the bag out. It was a new jacket, with a hood. She slowly unfolded it, looking serious. Her ex-husband, Dario, had bought clothes for her, too. He'd enjoyed choosing the way she dressed, buying her things that pleased him and him only. Thomas had picked up on a change in Sabina's mood—uncertain if she liked it or hated it. *He's replacing the clothes he helped ruin. It's a sweet gesture. He's not like Dario*, Sabina thought to herself. She broke out in a broad nervous smile.

"Thank you. I won't be cold now. What shall we do today?" She unfolded and tried on her new jacket.

Thomas was relieved. "Well, I was thinking of seeing the Hagia Sophia, then after lunch maybe having a nap. Also, I'd like to change the dressing on your shoulder before we go."

"Okay, it sounds like you've got a plan. Mind if I tag along?" Sabina hugged him.

Thomas accepted it with pleasure. She smelled fresh and looked truly passionate about their little trip. After a night out with his *dolls*, Sabina was a pure delight to talk to.

"There'd hardly be a point without you. Take the bag. We'll go to the room upstairs." Thomas slipped an arm around her waist.

In the room, Thomas carefully removed the dressing and examined the wound on Sabina's shoulder. It was swollen. *Fuck! That looks infected*, he thought to himself. *If this round of disinfectant doesn't fix the issue, then I'll have to get her antibi-otics.* He applied antiseptic cream, covering the wound again.

CHAPTER 11

HEAVEN AND EARTH

SABINA AND THOMAS slowly drove through Istanbul, the windscreens awash with rain, the sky darkened by low, ominous clouds. On the sidewalk, people flocked under a moving ceiling of umbrellas. The multicultural past of the city was reflected in each building, old estates sprawled next to the soaring towers of tomorrow; the cosmopolitan tourism showed in the diversity of the crowd; the people thronged in the plazas and shopfronts. Every structure reflected many influences, mostly those that came from Byzantine, Genoese, Ottoman, and modern Turkish sources. Sabina spied the Hagia Sophia in the distance—a piece of ancient history, staunchly remaining the same, even as the modern world flourished around it. Thomas managed to take the place of a car that was leaving, cutting off a van in the process. A corpulent man with a t-shirt made from an American flag leaned out of the van window and screamed through the rain.

"You crazy? Trying to get someone killed? You don't know how to drive, pridoorak!"

Sabina frowned. "Did he just say 'pridoorak?'"

"That is actually what I heard, too..."

"What does that mean?"

"I have no idea. I think it's Russian. Let's flee to the museum before he gets physical."

Sabina stepped out of the car, carefully opening her umbrella to avoid the rain, only to find that it was gone. The grey clouds were torn apart, and the sun was trickling down on the museum of Hagia, which turned from golden to silver. Sabina glanced back to find Thomas gazing at her with admiration.

"What's that look for?"

"I had the strongest feeling the rain stopped for you, my lady."

"Don't be silly, von Essen!"

They walked up flights of stairs in the parkland, then into a large forecourt. Visitors streamed through a grand archway. Some of them were locals—Sabina could see turbaned men and women with headscarves or veils, but most of the visitors were from all over the world, presenting an international display of fashions and accents. At a distance, the ancient structure looked much like many photos that Sabina had seen, but now it felt like a mountain thundering up before her. She smiled with nervous anticipation, walking hand-in-hand with her new love.

The massive building of Hagia Sophia was illuminated by golden lights that washed up the pale walls, setting them aglow through the greyness of the day. The most eye-catching part of the museum was the tremendous central dome. The first dome was planned as a circle but turned out to be an ellipse. It was supported by the arches between piers, which were unique. Sabina read about the dome in a tourist brochure at the hotel. She knew about forty windows encircled the base of the dome;

that's why she expected nothing but sun today. The view of the light floating around the church and gilded mosaics was surprisingly calming.

The walls of the hall were clad in exquisite cut marble with rich motionless patterns. Sabina could feel the weight of history settling on her. She shivered as the pathos of the place touched her being. She knew the history of this holy place. This city had been Byzantium to the Greeks, but Constantinople to the Roman emperor, who had built the first great Christian temple on this ground. It had been burned, sacked, rebuilt many times; each time grander than the last. This structure had stood since the sixth century, shining over the memory of former smaller temples, visions, wars, kings.

Sabina and Thomas finally passed through an ornamental arch, into the Sanctum. Her hand fell from his, and she walked dumbstruck out into the grand space of the next room. The floor was made of colossal paving stones, cut from a rippled marble that gave them the pattern of turquoise waves. Sabina turned her face upward, looking up to the sun. She felt like she was standing at the bottom of an enormous canyon. Dozens of windows pierced the chamber's base. The support between them was so slender; they seemed to melt in the rays of the light. Sabina was hurt by the feeling that this whole place was suspended from heaven rather than resting on earth. The complexity and mysteriousness of this ancient museum overwhelmed her. She was transfixed. Sabina could see old angelic figures depicted on the buttresses above her, flowing Islamic inscriptions on the walls, hailing back to the time when the building was reconstructed into a mosque. She wondered if Christians were angry that this aged palace had been converted to another faith, that crosses had been painted over and all murals covered. The brilliant ring of light seemed to set the dome in motion. Sabina sensed the presence of God in this place. She knew, deep in her core the building was alive. It was gazing into her soul from every angle. She felt stripped naked, even of flesh; at the same time, the building was stripped, too. The angels, the inscriptions—all fell away—leaving only motion that existed beyond the human illusion. She was looking at the truth, and it gazed back into her. She felt fear, shame, self-loathing, peace; everything she was meant to feel. She was a sinner, asking for forgiveness. Her lover was right next to her. *Her lover...*How could she help this man violate the Christian grave?!? Sabina shivered with guilt, but the light did not waver, nor the gaze falter. After a short walk, her fears and shame began to seem foolish. They were beneath the Lord, who did not care for triviality!

What do you want of me? she thought. The answer seemed plain, without any words spoken. *It* wanted to be admired, seen, known, loved. She could not shake the feeling that, somehow, she was connected to this place.

Thomas watched Sabina with slowly growing concern. He hoped that she would like the place. It would also be another way for him to gain her trust. He watched how Sabina had wandered into the Sanctum, how she'd been staring at it unresponsively for fifteen minutes. There were tears on her face. *Must be having a breakdown,* Thomas thought. *I guess the past few days are catching up with her.*

"Darling?" Thomas's voice scraped against the tapestry of Sabina's thoughts. She lowered her head and looked at him. Sabina's eyes were bright, her face luminous. Thomas felt as if she saw right through him, knew all his secrets. He was rooted to the spot, fearful—the girl looked like a witch.

"Are you okay, Tom? You look pale." Sabina took a step toward him.

"I'm fine. It's a wonderful place, isn't it?" His calm mask was back. He closed his eyes for a moment, put his head back, and drew a slow, deep breath.

"Indescribable. Thank you for bringing me here."

"I'm so glad you like it. I was going to look at some of the features outside. I can see you're bewildered and not ready to step out yet. Why don't I let you follow your heart? I'll come later to find you for lunch, okay?"

"Great idea."

Thomas left. He needed some time alone—time to reconcile with the way she had looked at him. He was not sure he dared to lie to her again. He quickly ran out to the fountain, whispering, 'bloody Sicilian witch.' Then he put on a calm smile, pulled on his rubber gloves, and prepared to check the setting.

Sabina wandered the hall, deeply absorbed in the exquisite details of the grand building. The Revetment was beautiful. Each piece of rippled marble had been cut carefully down the middle and opened up like the pages of a book: each panel had absolute symmetry. She began to see beyond the temple's splendor; she started to look inwards, at its scars. The floors were uneven from the wear of millions of feet. Some parts of the marble revetments were gone or had been painted instead. She gently touched the wall as if trying to heal the temple. Despite feeling surreal and giddy, Sabina found herself in a wonderful mood: she chatted with strangers, smiled, danced, and pirouetted when it pleased her. Some people stared, but she didn't care. When Sabina found men eyeing her shape, she accepted their admiration with a confidence she had never before managed. For some reason, this place made her feel free, sensual, alive. *If I told my father what I've felt in this place, he would drag me to the alter by my hair to pray until my knees bled*, she thought.

Suddenly, Sabina found herself in another hall, where a gaggle of people gathered around a pillar. Their interest drew her in. She saw a sign WISH COLUMN (Weeping Column). She had heard of this sacred pillar and its holy powers to heal. Sabina had preferred the title 'Weeping.' As the legend says, the moistness of the pillar was the tears of the Virgin Mary. She rounded the column. She saw a tentative Asian woman from the gaggle step forward and place her thumb in a hole on one side of the pillar. The area around the hole was worn from touching. Sabina thought it looked reminiscent of an eye. The woman retreated, and a man stepped forward. He also placed his thumb in the hole...Sabina joined the queue, waiting for her turn. Each person rotated their thumb around, before pressing it to the chest or where they wanted to be healed. It was Sabina's turn. She recalled the legend about Emperor Constantine, who had discovered the pillars' extraordinary power. He had been wandering the halls with a terrible headache, leaned his head upon the pillar, and found himself cured. Instead of the following tradition with a thumb, Sabina gently leaned her injured shoulder against the pillar and held it, eyes closed. The metal was cold and moist to touch. A man's voice, nasal, with an English accent, came from nowhere, "I don't mean to be rude, but you're supposed to put your finger in this hole. It's because a group of faithful Muslims once went to pray, but the building wasn't facing Kaaba, which is a thing for them, and then Dues Ex Machina appeared and was going to turn the whole building but was seen by a pilgrim and so had to vanish.

So yeah, that's why you rotate your thumb in the hole. Are you even listening?"

Sabina drew back from the bronze and gave the man a weak understanding smile. With some surprise, she noticed the pillar had changed. Now it was covered in beads of red moisture, drops of which trickled down its surface. Tourists around her had seen that, too: some were fearful, others— excited. Exclamations and discussions burst forth; a few started photographing the change. Sabina backed away, not wanting to be near the babbling. She turned into a vaulted antechamber, displaying a huge urn.

Thomas was standing and looking at the urn. He felt Sabina's touch, looked back, and said, "There you are! I hope you had fun."

"Yeah, it feels like I'm in another world."

"I suppose in a way, you are. I've found a nice place for lunch. It's well past midday."

Sabina looked around, not wanting to leave.

"You know, you can come here every day, or even later today if you want to," Thomas explained.

"True. Where are we eating?"

"A stone's throw from here, the Matbah Restaurant. It has nice views."

They left arm-in-arm out of the far side of the building. It was windy and chilly, but the rain had not returned. They crossed a paved yard surrounded by trees. The centerpiece of the yard was an old ornate fountain, crested by a stonefish. Thomas stopped for one minute to admire the sculpture. Half a block away from the Sogku Cesme Square, they found a narrow three-story restaurant, nestled amongst a tangle of flats and shops. They seated, ordered food, and enjoyed the view of the beautiful city.

"Have you been to the Hagia Sophia before?" asked Sabina.

"Eight years ago. I worked on a small dig in the area. You seemed to connect with the place."

"Yes. What an astonishing museum! Don't you think it's a perfect symbol of the transformation of the physical into the spiritual? Do you feel it lift you and change you?"

"I know what you mean. The whole building has been made to impress awe and sovereignty on those within it. But I don't think I felt what you did, Sabina." Thomas chewed his lip.

"I feel as though...I feel certain...that I saw God. I was in his presence. We spoke, but without words" Sabina said, studying Thomas's face. He looked attentive and a little troubled.

"Why not? What better place to experience an epiphany, right? I'm humbled to be a part of the journey which led you here, my wonderful Sicilian friend."

Thomas caught sight of Odette down the street. He felt the hot pressure of blood gripping his brain. It couldn't be happening. That girl was insane.

"Only a friend?" Sabina smiled at his mention, living in her own world.

They ate their meal—chicken kebabs and baked mushrooms, with the chef's recommendation of wine. Across the street, an ice cream vendor in a green turban performed tricks with ice cones, flipping and spinning them, somehow dropping none. Sabina watched the scene full of joy. Thomas watched the woman in the crowd, wearing a white dress, a big beige hat, and holding a *Psychologies* magazine. After lunch, the staff thanked them and asked to come again.

"Of course! What a wonderful place," promised Sabina.

"Agreed. You know that wine has gone straight to my head, Darling. I wouldn't mind heading back to the hotel for a nap."

"A nap at your age?" she teased.

"A manly nap," he said with mock indignation. "If you want to stay, I can…"

"No, you're right. We've got plenty of time."

Sabina pondered how terrified of lurking shooters she had been when she debarked the flight from Germany, how distant and unreal all that felt now. Should she still be worried? She could not decide.

After a short drive, they arrived at their hotel, parked at the back of the building. They walked inside and took the elevator upstairs. Almost at once, Thomas climbed into bed. Sabina undressed, casting teasing and promising smiles. Thomas watched her in silence. He felt… intimidated. He was still shaken from the way she had looked at him in the Sanctum of the Hagia Sophia. He hadn't overcome the fear he'd felt there. Sabina cast the sheets off Thomas, crawling on top of him. She bit his neck, pressing her warm body closer. It could not be more evident that she wanted to make love and assumed that he did, too. But he did not… He was too anxious about his secret mission. He was too troubled and fearful of this woman who seemed so compelling. He also promised Lifen that he wouldn't fuck his new Sicilian doll. He had to say "no." He had to make an excuse, but he couldn't find the courage or the words. In that particular moment, Thomas remembered all the women who hadn't *really* been in the mood to sleep with him —how he'd cuddled and coaxed his way into their panties, knowing they were only half willing. He always thought that half willing is enough. Now he felt like one of them.

Sabina's hand slipped down into Thomas's boxers, only to find him flaccid. She pulled his boxers off and started working on his soft boy. First, with her hand, then, her mouth, always maintaining eye contact. It was only a matter of time before

Thomas's body responded—he was a man after all. She climbed on top of him, gazing down into his eyes, pressing him deep inside her. Thomas played along, hands on her hips, eyes closed.

Afterward, he rolled on the other side of the bed, wrestling with what he was feeling.

"Are you okay, Thomas?"

"Yes. I'm just tired."

She cradled him. It felt strange to be embraced by the one whom he planned to hurt. Thomas slipped into troubled dreams.

Thomas must be exhausted. He's usually a lot more playful, like a hurricane, thought Sabina. *I'm not tired at all. What am I going to do with my afternoon? Shopping? Yes, I'll go shopping. After all, I don't have any souvenirs yet!*

Sabina kissed Thomas while he slept, dressed, and strolled downstairs. She took the car. After checking travel guides on her phone (she realized before that the city had a bewildering number of regions with very different looks and feels), she headed to a section of the old town, where a rambling Grand Bazaar was offering everything from fruits to watches.

She parked her car and slipped into the crowd. It was fascinating how the old world mingled with the new, without any conflict. Some Turks wore traditional dress, hijab, and headscarves, whereas others dressed much like Europeans. Sabina browsed, looking at garments, steel, ceramics, candles. A Turkish man in a golden turban beckoned her to the mouth of his small shop. It sold swords, knives, watches, and vibrant traditional clothes. Sabina came forward.

"Madam, I can see you are looking for something special."

She smiled, "I'm not sure what I'm looking for."

"See here!" he produced a heavily curved dagger. "This is a Hançer—a ceremonial blade, a powerful symbol of Istanbul. They are a popular souvenir; some are ornamental, in various sizes and colours. I have others of the finest quality if you'd like to check."

"They're traditionally only worn by men, aren't they?"

"True, but maybe you have a special man that you know who deserves such a gift. Or maybe... well, time changes, everything changes."

"Can I see some of these blades of quality that you mentioned?"

She settled at length on a Damascus Hançer, curved and ornate, with both handle and sheath plated in embossed silver. Sabina ignored the price. *Thomas will like it. I'll give it to him when we decide to fly back to Germany, as a memory, the bond of our love,* she thought.

Sabina headed back to the hotel in hopes that Thomas was awake, but she found their room empty. A lone note sat on the dining table: 'Went to meet an old friend. I'll be back after dark.' Sabina frowned. The note seemed abrupt. She had a creeping feeling something was coming between Thomas and her, but she had no idea what. She also had the evening to herself. *I'll go back to the Hagia Sophia. It's open for another hour and a half, then I'll meet Thomas here, after dinner.*

She changed her clothes, slipping into a knee-length black dress with a print of white lilies. She drove through the same streets, looking up from time to time at the temperamental weather brewing above. Soon she found parking, took her handbag, making her way to the high arch of the Hagia Sophia, which was still glowing with golden radiance. When she entered, a security officer added, "One hour only, ma'am."

She returned to the Sanctum to find it changed—the inner space illuminated by dozens of electric chandeliers. The exquisite cavern seemed like heaven from the dark and troublesome world beyond. An hour vanished. Sabina heard an announcement echoing over speakers, asking visitors in the museum to make their way to the exits. With a sigh, she walked through the halls towards the nearest door with a trickle of other tourists. Almost near the exit, she heard a great rendering, alarmingly loud, followed by the tearing or breaking of rock. Looking around, Sabina realized the sound must have carried from outside, probably, from the old courtyard. Her inner voice of caution was drowned out by the shrillness of her curiosity. Gathering her courage, the beautiful Sicilian woman hurried towards the crazy sound.

CHAPTER 12

FOUR BROKEN HOPES

HURRYING THROUGH THE VAST HALLS, Sabina found herself spilling out of an archway into one of the rear court-yards. She knew she had been here earlier today. She could see the ancient fountain, a stonefish at its top, spurting a thin column of water skyward. The only problem was that the fountain was ruined now—its whole side torn away, the massive chunk of masonry held by iron spikes and chains, attached to a black cargo van. She noticed a strange emblem on the cargo's side, with the words "Byzantine Treasures." A couple of dark figures in balaclavas worked around the fountain. A slim silhouette in black unhitched the chain from the van. Another backed up the van. A tall, athletic woman in jeans and a brown leather coat jumped out of the vehicle's back doors when a jackhammer stopped hefting. She fixed the problem, beginning to work on the exposed foundation of the fountain. Stone was exploding everywhere. No water escaped the fountain, despite the rock being torn away. The next two figures by the fountain shocked Sabina. One was a lean man in a grey fitted suit. Despite the balaclava, Sabina could tell it was her Thomas. She knew his shape. By his side stood a woman in a long rose-colored dress, similar to hers in the cut. Sabina felt replaced, betrayed, confused. Before she had time to reconcile her feelings, the rattling tone of the jackhammer changed distinctly metallic. The tall woman stopped, shouting, "Yes!!!" She grabbed a small pick, working at the ruined stone. Thomas helped her.

Movement outside of the scene caught Sabina's eye. From where she stood, elevated by a broad flight of marble stairs, she could see down into the grounds. She saw four police officers in riot vests: two were armed with submachine guns, another two with pistols. They were running up into the courtyard. Sabina could tell that neither Thomas nor his mysterious companions knew that the police force was already here. Panic ceased Sabina. She had no time to figure out her feelings. They were going to shoot her lover, her Thomas!

"Lookout, it's the police! They've got guns!" she blurted. Thomas whirled around.

"Oh God! Why is she here?" he shouted.

"Listen, everybody! Police are here! We've got to go!" said the blonde athletic woman.

"Get the box! It's our only chance...Out! Out!" Thomas shook under the stress of emotions.

Madison looked at the partly uncovered box set under the ancient granite. She grabbed up the jackhammer and stabbed the container with all her strength. She levered it out violently with an explosion of rock. Sabina had stumbled to a halt near the fountain, staring at what was happening. Around the courtyard's edge, a group of three tourists stood staring, pointing at them. One took photos.

"Come with us, Sabina! I'll explain later, I swear," Thomas grabbed the box with both hands and wrestled it free of the rubble. He ran with two women to the black van. Sabina followed them.

The police made it to the top of the stairs, shouting something in Turkish. The short woman in black jeans took out a semiautomatic and leveled three shots at their side. It was loud and messy. Sabina screamed. One of the officers fell to his knees, clutching his riot vest; the other three returned fire. The air filled with the terrifying bark of guns, punctuated by the crack of pistols. The tourists were gone. The short woman fired again. She placed her foot on the tow-ball to vault into the van and then collapsed, the gun falling from her hand.

"NINAAA!" the blonde screamed in fear. She leaned out of the van, grabbed Nina's arm, and hauled her shuddering body up, into the back. Thomas slammed the doors. There were no windows. In the front seat, fine-dressed Odette was babbling something in French. She looked back, in tears, asking in broken English, "Madison, is Nina shot? What's happening?!?"

"Drive, bitch! Now!!" yelled Thomas.

Odette punched the accelerator; the car began roaring down into the grounds. Madison was holding Nina's body. She had pulled off her balaclava, watching how the small Russian woman was gasping for breath, blood bubbling out of her mouth—flesh pale, eyes wide, lips in sweat.

"Fuck! Someone get me a first aid kit!" yelled Madison.

"Won't help. She needs a hospital," answered Thomas in a sad voice.

Sabina sat in the corner, pressed against the wall, watching the panic in horror. The Russian woman had half a dozen bleeding holes in her torso. The blood was trickling onto the dirty floor. The sounds of submachine guns returned, thundering, just as the van began rattling down the stairs, then the road. Holes sprang into the walls, with light streaming through it. Thomas looked shocked for a moment, then reeled drunkenly as blood exploded off his head, spraying Sabina's face and dress. He fell, motionless, across the dying Russian. Thomas's head landed on Sabina's lap. She grasped his shoulders, staring down at his head. It was twisted—a hole punched in his skull, with oozed brains and blood. The once handsome face of her lover was now slack, scary, made grotesque by death.

Odette began maneuvering through trees, swearing in French. Lifen, the third woman, pulled off her balaclava and slumped against a wall—her beautiful Asian face in pain, shocked. Madison growled, and heaved Thomas's corpse off Nina. She cradled Nina's body in her arms. The Russian tried to speak but couldn't, her mouth gaping wordlessly.

"Don't try, don't try, just breathe, Nina, breath!" stammered Madison.

They were in the streets now, driving as fast as they could. Sabina could hear honking horns, the revving of the engine; the van swerved left and right. Nina gave a horrible shudder and slumped still. Her open eyes were staring, unfocused, at the roof.

"Nina?!? Nina?? Noooooo!" screamed Madison in despair.

Odette turned her head around. She saw not only Nina's limp body being cradled in Madison's arms, but also Thomas, splattered in blood. She screamed. The car shuddered with the sound of screeching metal and splintering glass.

"Did we just fuckin' crash?" yelled Lifen.

"No. We clipped a car. Oh God! Are they both dead? Thomas?"

"They're dead," Madison's voice from the back was dangerously cold.

"Do you hear the sirens, Oddie?"

Sabina hadn't, but now, when it had been said, the wailing keen of pursuing sirens cut through her consciousness.

"They outnumber us. They know the city," Madison continued. "When they catch us, add that we've shot a cop, plus defaced a national monument... What do you think they'd do? If we fight, they're going to kill us all. If we manage to surrender or survive the beating, we're going to be in a Turkish jail. And France doesn't give a shit about you, Odette! You're a wanted fuckin' thief! If you don't focus and outsmart those assholes, we are screwed! Are you hearing me? Do it for Thomas!"

"All right. All right. Let me drive... Odette's voice quivered as she spoke.

The van sped through the streets. Sabina had no idea where they were going or how Odette hoped to allude the smaller nimbler police cars in the hulking van.

Sabina lifted her eyes from the corpses to check her new living companions—all complete strangers. The Asian woman in the green cocktail dress was sending text messages on her phone, focused, but very scared. The French girl was blubbering a song, driving with evident skill through the crowded streets of Istanbul. Sabina had no idea how they hadn't crashed yet. She looked over at the athletic woman, in the leather jacket, who was covered in Nina's blood—a little bit stuck on her neck, but the balaclava soaked up the worst. The hair of the young woman was dyed platinum blonde; she looked like a fitness model from a cheap fashion magazine.

"This is your fault. Look at this fucking mess," Madison said, staring at Sabina.

Sabina felt anger twist in her guts. This blonde was bigger than her, but she didn't care. Sabina's hand went into her handbag and drew out the Turkish knife. She threw herself at

Madison, her headlong assault, driving her against the wall. Madison grabbed Sabina's jacket, growling. She was about to throw Sabina off, when she froze, feeling the curved blade tickling her throat.

The mad Sicilian woman spoke in a hiss, "My fault? I don't even know who you are, but that's my lover! He is dead, on the floor. From where I'm standing, it looks like all of you got him killed!"

Lifen slipped her phone into the small Bottega Veneta handbag. She held out both hands, wobbling, as the car screeched around a corner. Odette was still swearing in French.

"Sabina, we know who you are. We were all friends of Thomas. Please, put the knife away. Look at all the blood. No more, okay? We need to watch each other's backs. I promise we are not your enemies," Lifen explained.

Sabina looked at the Asian woman, jaw clenched.

Madison said with her hands up, "She is right. I'm sorry. That was stupid. You did nothing wrong. I'm just pissed off! Nina was part of our team."

Sabina pulled the knife away and sat on the floor near Thomas.

"Okay," said Lifen. "I've got a way out of this. There's a small private plane at the airport. It's corporate, belongs to my father. He believes something different is happening...Yeah, yeah, I lied. The most important...the plane can fly us anywhere we need to go."

Madison shook her head. "We can't just drive to the airport. People at the hotel know Sabina's face. Some tourists took pictures of us at the fountain. How are we going to get to that plane?"

"I've lost them for a minute!" laughed Odette. "Seems they've got a helicopter in the air now. Shit, I'm never going to shake them again. We need to change cars. I can easily jack this one... She nodded to a bulky BMW sitting in a narrow brick alley, under the ark.

"That's a BMW. Won't it be hard to crack?" asked Sabina.

"It was made in 2008, girl. I can get into it, no problem," said Odette, scowling. She stopped, quickly climbed out of the car, and hurried over to the BMW.

"We have to take their bodies," ordered Lifen. "At least that car has a big boot. Here," she handed Sabina a small packet of wet wipes from her handbag. "You've got his blood on your face. Clean it up."

Sabina had wiped her face and stumbled out of the back of the van. Odette had the boot up on the BMW. Cars trickled past the ends of the alley, the flats all around them blared out the sound of televisions. Madison and Sabina lifted Thomas, placing him in the boot of the new car. Lifen shifted over bags, grabbed the bronze box, leaving the old van. The last one was Nina. Madison went back, tenderly lifting Nina's tiny body. Odette started spraying the blood in the van with a small blue bottle. Madison was a few steps from the BMW when the back door to one of the flats opened, and a tired-looking woman stepped out, thumbing a cigarette out of a packet. She stood frozen a couple of seconds, taking in the scene before her. "Heeeelppppp!"

Lifen quickly walked forward, speaking Turkish. "Please, don't scream, help us! We've had an accident. The girl is hurt. Can we use your phone?"

Before the startled woman could answer, Lifen pressed a taser into her ribs. The woman stiffened, staggered, and collapsed. Lifen electrocuted her again, just in case, then dragged the body into the house.

Madison placed Nina's corpse in the boot. Odette climbed in to drive, preparing to leave.

"Is our van clean?" asked Lifen from her seat.

"Yes and no. I've sprayed the blood with some crap like pneumonia. Believe me, you don't want to know what it is. It will keep the police away from our scent for a while, but Sabina is not wearing our gloves, so...," explained Odette.

"Okay, dummies, let's drive. At least this car has tinted windows." Lifen waved her hand to the road.

Sabina opened her handbag, looking for the Bible. It wasn't there. She hid her face in the palms of her hands, whispering, *Look, God, at how distressed I am; all my insides are churning. My heart is troubled within me because I vigorously rebelled. Outside the sword brings loss of life, while at home death rules.*

CHAPTER 13

TRUST AND BETRAYAL

ODETTE CRUISED through the tangled streets of Istanbul, listening to how sirens wined far away in the distance.

"I assume you have a plan to get us where we need to be, Odette?" asked Lifen.

"*Qui*, but nothing fancy. I'm going to get us clothes, then take care of the bodies," she hesitated, trembling. "After that, we'll drive out to the airport. The men who work for your father can bluff us through better than we can. I think you should talk to them."

"Sure, I'll tell them." Lifen opened her phone again.

"I'm listening to the police radio," Odette gestured to her ear. "If the car's called in as missing, we're going to have to switch wheels again, and fast."

"I think we should drop Nina's body near the local hospital," said Madison, whose anger seemed to have melted into sadness.

"What for? She is dead!" answered Lifen. For a moment stillness and quietness surrounded her seat. She glanced at

Madison, changing her decision. Peace was the best way to keep the situation under control.

"Of course! Bad call, sorry. I'm too stressed," Lifen continued typing her message.

Odette pulled over in empty paid parking, fed coins into the meter, and sauntered into a clothing shop to emerge with bulging bags. She climbed into the car, buckled her seat belt, and announced, "We can change in that parking lot if none of you have a better idea."

"There is a garage at my hotel. It's out the back, private, often empty. I recall it's got a tap and hose, which could be useful," said Sabina.

There was a silence as everyone considered the plan.

"Is there any way they could trace Sabina that quickly to her hotel even if they knew who she was?" asked Madison, glancing between Lifen and Odette.

"Are you booked in under your name?" said Lifen.

"Ah, no. We were Mr. and Mrs. Knopf," Sabina sighed.

"I don't see how they could know, not yet. Even if they do get a good picture of you, it will take time. Let's use that garage," as usual, Lifen made the decision.

Thirty minutes later, the girls were scrubbed clean of blood and dressed in fresh clothes. Everything they were previously wearing was packed in a black bag. Given little privacy, washing with a hose next to the car, Sabina noted that her partners in crime took note of her birthmark. She wanted to check the dressing on her shoulder but felt too tired. Plus, the air had been filled with a lot of curiosity and questions. It hadn't bled through the dressing; that's all that matter.

The mysterious box from Hagia Sophia—*the reason that all of this had happened*—was wrapped carefully in a large scarf and placed in a padded satchel. It remained unopened. Madison silently volunteered to shoulder the gruesome task of wrapping the two corpses and dropping them near the closest hospital or clinic. Sabina was glad she didn't have to help. Everyone was tense as Odette drove out along the brightly lit highway towards the airport. Sabina held the satchel containing the sacred box on her lap. It was awkwardly bulky. Lifen spoke in Korean on her phone. Madison listened to music, crying.

When they arrived at the airport, Odette pulled off the main road. She drove up to a private gate. Sabina nervously let the padded satchel slide down into the footwell, out of sight. There was a security booth looming on the right side of the car, cameras staring down on them. They stopped, facing a closed steel gate.

The booth was staffed by two stern men in security uniforms. They were talking to three men in expensive suits. One of Korean descent, dressed in a blue silk suit, tapped his watch, gesturing through the closed gate where several small private jets waited for boarding. The security officer seemed put-upon: he was looking between the Korean fella and the car with the girls, trying to make a decision. Finally, he relented, holding up his hands in a placating gesture. He took a fat envelope and pressed the button to open the gate.

Sabina sat, scared to make a move. The BMW drove through the gate, following the three businessmen, who had all climbed into a golf cart. They drove up to a small private jet.

As the car pulled up, Lifen said, "Act casual, don't rush too much. We don't want security to get suspicious of anything."

No one argued. The Korean man in the blue suit came over, smiling professionally. He opened Lifen's door, bowing,

"Ms. Ong, welcome to your flight. Shall we get your baggage?"

"We don't have much, Asha. We'll wait on board."

Sabina noted, with some awe, how well Lifen slipped into the role of spoiled elegance. She stepped out of the car like a real movie star. Everyone else followed. The jet was luxurious inside: twelve beige seats in swivelling lounges next to tinted oval windows. A single thick-necked European man in a grey suit stood in the cabin, a tattoo of a dragon's head peeked above the collar of his satin shirt. He smiled as they took their seats.

Sabina played with the button controls. She tried to change the position of the chair to face the window. She watched how two other men carried heavy boxes from the car to the plane to load them. Her eyes flicked up when the unknown vehicle slid out of the darkness into the bright light, illuminating the road. It moved toward the jet. Sabina's throat tightened; a cold sick feeling washed through her. She recognized a police car.

"Oh, God! It's a police car!" she stammered.

"I see them," Lifen said coldly. "Stay put. Our men can take care of it."

Sabina sat in a state of panic, watching in horror as the gate slid open and the police car sped through. It parked next to their stolen BMW. Two police officers climbed out. They approached the Asian men in suits. Sabina could only see Asha, who politely walked over to the police officers, offering his hand. The officer didn't shake the hand. Instead, he pointed to the stolen BMW behind him, speaking aggressively. They chatted for a couple of minutes, then the second policeman called the other two men forward, showing them the car. The businessmen were trying to talk the police down; they tapped their watches, gesturing at the plane. It was clear the police weren't listening. They shouted something to Asha, one of the officers fondling his pistol.

OMG. They're going to search them and then they're going to come on board! I'll go to prison for something I didn't do! thought Sabina, trying to find ways to fix the situation.

"Just a minute," said the towering man from the cabin. He walked over to the hatch, stepped out on top of the stairs, and shouted in a cheerful voice, "Hey guys! How do you want your coffee?"

The police turned, surprised. At that moment, all three Korean men drew pistols out of their shoulder holsters and repeatedly fired at open targets—eight sharp bangs. The officers collapsed on the runway. Sabina clamped her hand over her mouth to stop herself from screaming.

Asha walked up to check the bodies. He stood there, with his glossy black shoes, shoulder-width apart, chromed pistol glinting in his hand. Sabina was hyperventilating. Asha had turned from a smiling cute businessman into an assassin in a few minutes. Sabina's brain was having trouble keeping up... one of the officers was utterly still. The second, amazingly, despite three holes in his chest, was contorted in a pool of his blood, trying to draw his gun. Asha slowly aimed the gun at his forehead. He fired. Sabina saw how the head of the officer snapped back: he slumped still. Sabina stared through a tinted window, unable to look away. Her hand still over her mouth, in case her body tried to scream.

Asha walked away but then changed his mind. He went back and shot the other officer in the head, too—the one who didn't move at all. Satisfied with the result, Asha shouted to his companions. All three strolled to the jet.

Sabina could see the small figures of technicians in yellow overalls attending the landing gear of one of the airliners on the other side of the forecourt. They were frozen, still, staring. Four officers from the security booth spilled through the gate, running over on foot. Sabina could feel panic starting to rise in her body. Soon the whole police force will be after them! They can't get away with this!

Sabina rotated her chair away from the window, took deep breaths, and tried to calm her nerves. Of all her new companions, only Lifen was watching the scene. She looked coldly nonchalant. Odette gave Sabina a sympathetic look, while she held a glass of champagne. Sabina focused on how collected all girls were and drew strength from it.

Asha opened the door to the pilot's cabin, giving the order, "Let's get in the air fast, but keep it low." He turned back to Lifen and added, "Where are we heading, Ms. Ong?"

"Give us ten minutes. I'll tell you in the air."

Asha and his two companions stepped into the cabin. They hauled the door closed behind them. The plane began to move, trucking slowly along the forecourt. It began to speed up as it angled for a stretch of open space. Sabina was certain; it wasn't a legal runway, maybe partly forecourt or driveway, cutting diagonally across two other tracks.

Three men sat down, waiting as the craft sped up. With a lurch, the plane soared up into the stormy night sky. Sabina could only imagine that the pilots must be getting frantic radio calls for taking off so randomly. She could see the blinking lights of other aircraft in the black sky. The moment was surreal. It dawned on her—her whole life she had followed the rules, and she had always been surrounded by those who did the same. Even the corrupt police, God, or Sicilian Mafia had strict rules, but these people who were sitting around her right now, crushed all laws under their feet. She found the idea dangerously liberating. Asha rotated his chair to face Lifen and asked again, "Where are we going, Ms. Ong?"

"I told your gorillas, Asha, give us ten minutes of privacy, and I'll tell you."

"Of course, Ms. Ong, you are the boss. We'll wait up the back." Asha gestured at a narrow red curtain next to the latrine. He stood up and walked down the back into the rear area. Two other men followed him.

"Are you okay, Sabina? Relax!" Lifen looked at her with concern.

"I'm okay. I was just surprised."

"Good. Listen up, everybody! First, we need to decide where to go. Second, we no longer have a leader. Third, we can't keep this plane so low... but one thing at a time. The most important... we need a place to hide, somewhere safe."

"I've got nothing; this is the wrong part of the world for me," replied Madison.

"I'd need time. I don't know. Let me think," said Odette, clearly at a loss.

Sabina looked up from her feet. She mumbled, "I've got a place."

Lifen looked amazed. "Where is it? Run it past us."

"We're going to Italy. Obviously, we don't fly over Greece. We fly west over the Sea of Marmara, then South into the Aegean Sea, around the southern extent of Greece, then north, into the Ionian Sea, past Albania, and into the Adriatic Sea." Sabina paused, catching a breath, then continued, "In this way, we are flying away from daybreak, which is to our advantage. We fly over Italy at about two-thirty in the morning. Touch down should be somewhere on the road, in a rural town, preferably east of Naples. We disembark. What was in the boxes?"

"Bodies." Lifen placed a finger to her lips.

"Bodies???" all three asked.

Odette sat bewildered: the shock from Thomas's death was still too strong to handle. Sabina suggested dropping the bodies to the bottom of the Adriatic.

"I have a contact. It can't be traced to me because I met him only a couple of days ago. I know he'd let us stay. We have to lay low before we figure out what to do next."

"Shit Sabina! You really thought that through!" said Madison.

"Your contact is rock solid? He won't crack if he'll see your face on the news?" repeated Lifen, looking at the Sicilian with an appraising eye.

Sabina was entirely unsure, but she wanted to be useful to these dangerous women. She answered without any pause, "I'm dead certain."

CHAPTER 14

THE RISING QUEEN

THE PLANE SWEPT over the fields of the mainland. Sabina looked out, feeling like the craft sailed out over the dark waters of the Marmara. It was flying so low that she thought they might land. The men were trying to sleep. Four women silently moved to the back of the plane, into the small kitchenette to discuss business. Odette made coffee. She was looking for sweets when she came across the first aid kit.

"Do you want me to change the dressing on your shoulder, Sabina?" Odette asked.

"Oh, thanks. I was so distracted I had forgotten about it."

Odette uncovered Sabina's shoulder and peeled off the plaster. Her face was puzzled, "Um, Sabina, you're all healed up..."

"Really?"

"Didn't you only get shot a few days ago?" asked Madison, craning her neck to see the pink skin of Sabina's healed shoulder. She pushed Lifen on the side, winking.

"So what? She's a fast healer," said Lifen with annoyance.

"We've got other things to discuss. Things that cannot wait! I mentioned before, we have no leader. We're carrying a hot potato box worth a fortune, but don't have a buyer. One of us will almost certainly have a chase after them," she looked sternly at Sabina.

"Yet, we need to stick together if we're going to get anything out of this crappy situation," Madison said, folding her arms.

Odette looked inside of the empty cup. She quickly poured more coffee, adding her comment, "I might find buyers on the dark web, but I'd need time. I doubt we'll get the price we're looking for."

"Okay. First things first," Lifen took the lead. "We need to decide who's the leader of the group. To discuss shit is fine, but in the end, we've all got different methods. I think that criminals can't be democrats."

Madison smiled and spoke up, "For me, it depends. If this is for a few weeks while we find a buyer, then one of you can take the reins. I believe I'm the only one who can't sell that damn *thing*. If we're sticking together to become a team—for profit, further work, protection—I'm keen to run the show. I've got lots of ideas."

"Good point, Mad! What do you think?" asked Lifen looking from face to face.

"An all-female team is too good to pass up, really," replied Odette with a hopeful smile. "I'm in for the long hall!"

"Why not? Me, too," Madison was thrilled: she immediately started to think of a name for her group, as well as their next job.

"I think the team works for me, too. It would have been better with Nina. That Russian had skills and contacts. We could have used it right now, but whatever. I'm willing to form a new group. Fresh start! Cheers!" Lifen filled her cup with wine.

All three girls looked at Sabina. Sabina kept her cool, but inside she was conflicted. From one side, she felt ill-equipped to start a life of crime. From the other side, she was inexplicably drawn to it. After her experience at the Hagia Sophia, she could not shake the feeling that God accepted her as she is. She got an idea that this, somehow, was a part of His big plan. She didn't feel guilt at all, only power and thirst to continue her dangerous path. The girls were starting to exchange glances; she decided to speak.

"I'm interested. I think we can sell this item. I'm keen to continue our sisterhood," that expression made the women smile. "But what we need to decide now is...who can lead the group?"

"Let's draw straws," said Odette. "Whoever gets a long one is the boss-lady from then on. Organized crime, babes!"

The others nodded in agreement.

"Okay. Who wants to take the reins, girls?" Lifen continued. "I do. I'd love to, but I think you all know that already."

"I kind of wouldn't mind ruling this boat, too," interrupted Odette, with a nervous laugh.

"I would like to be Queen Bee," said the forgotten Sicilian from her chair.

"Seems we all want to be in control. Let's draw straws to find out who's the one. I'm afraid it won't stick, though. It's easy to promise pink castles now when we've got a twenty-five percent chance of being in charge, but what about later? What stops someone from getting disgruntled or bailing?"

Lifen shook her head, "It's wrong to bail. We know too much; each of us is a liability. If you're going to draw, you've got to follow the rules. I'd say so: if someone doesn't stick with the organization or follow the orders, then we'll kill them. If you defect or disobey, you die."

"Harsh," said Madison, eyebrows up.

"You are scaring me, Lin," Odette looked at the Asian woman with worry.

Lifen pushed Odette to her chair, giving her a cold gaze, "You've got nothing to worry about. I'll ask Asha to prepare the straws. Rule number one: we'll draw at the same time."

Madison gave both thumbs up. Lifen took a fist full of red striped straws from the kitchen drawer and walked down the aisle to Asha. Two minutes later, Asha approached them, looking serious. He held out his hand with seven straws in it. He had pulled a black napkin around his hand; it was impossible to see the lower half of the straws.

He spoke up, "Each of you take hold of a straw."

Odette jumped up in excitement, looking hopeful.

"Draw your straw! Now!" continued Asha.

All four women lifted their hands at the same time. Asha stepped back and walked off, laughing.

At first, the four heads looked at their straws, then started comparing it. Odette was pouting—her straw was only two centimeters long! A few seconds later, as straws were held side-by-side, it was apparent that only one was the longest by a notable margin. The straw that Sabina Ferrara held.

Sabina's first order was to locate more alcohol, to celebrate the new organization. After two bottles of champagne, the girls were much more relaxed. They lounged in chairs at the rear of the plane, far less caring of being overheard by the sleepy men or Asha. Alcohol helped to calm Sabina's nerves. Drinking gave her time to gather her thoughts. She wasn't stupid—she could see the disappointment on her companion's faces. Regardless of that, being a queen of a criminal group still felt unreal, even shocking.

Eventually, Lifen spoke, "Well, Sabina, you're in charge. I suppose this organization needs a name and some rules."

"I'm still pondering a name..." said Sabina sheepishly. She hadn't, in fact, given it any thought.

"I know!" Odette was a little drunk, "We should call it Awesome Slaying Sirens!"

"Or Awesome Super Souls?" asked Madison with a laugh, playing along.

"No way! The acronym for that is ASS!" Lifen refused to accept the name.

"We do have nice asses!" giggled Odette.

"There's four of us. Let's make it 4ASS," said Sabina grinning, partly to agree, slightly to annoy Lifen.

"You can't be serious!" lamented the rich Asian, looking genuinely aghast. "What about the *miracle-gang*, or *ching wuan hung boo*?"

Sabina laughed, feeling dizzy from newfound power, "I prefer 4ASS, Lin. Who drew the long straw, huh?"

"Hurrah!" howled Odette, thrusting her empty glass towards the ceiling, "4ASS forever!"

"Fine! I can't believe this, but fine! If you bitches wish...," Lifen rolled her eyes.

"My rules are simple," Sabina stood up near her chair, preparing to give a long speech. "What I say is the law. That's the point, right? You can protest, but only once. Just once! After that, if you want to keep protesting, you can do it from the bottom of the sea—dead." She watched her team growing frightful. They looked at each other in disbelief. Sabina enjoyed the pause. "That's how samurai served their masters, girls. I've always admired it. It's a good middle ground between unswerving obedience and democracy. Next, no boyfriends or serious commitments outside of the organization. No pregnancy. Lovers are fine. I'm not saying you can't live life to the fullest, but I can't have any of you wandering off or stopping to raise kids. It's basically leaving the organization in disguise. Means you are dead to us. All make sense so far?"

The three women nodded. Odette looked upset, mostly about the boyfriends-rule.

Madison smiled and thumbed to Sabina's shoulder, "Don't worry. I've got a great dildo in my pocket. I can't hold down a relationship to save myself."

Sabina shook her head in agreement, "Last, all the money 4ASS makes, after the expenses of the organization and investments in travel, gear and food, will be split evenly between the four of us. I'm greedy, and so are you. Let's be greedy together."

"Wow, I like the last one!" said Odette, brightening up.

"It won't apply to those we hire, employ, or add to the organization later. Those will be dealt with on a case-by-case basis. Their pay will essentially be our expenses. We are the inner circle. We are the team!"

Madison uncorked the third bottle of champagne, spilling some on the carpet. She topped up everyone's glasses, smiling, "To great leaders and lots of money!"

The four women clinked their glasses together, drank, and danced. Sabina took a couple of pictures. Madison sat with Asha, chatting about guns and cars. At that moment, Odette took Sabina's hand, leading her to the quiet corner. She whispered in her ear, "Something that's been worrying me is your phone, Sabina. It's only a matter of time before Interpol is going to use the number to locate us. We should ditch it as soon as possible. I'm sorry I forgot to mention it before, with all the deaths. Also, you might want to give your new identity some thought. I'm going to arrange fake IDs next month. In the meanwhile, you shouldn't walk around, calling yourself Sabina Ferrara."

With a sigh, Sabina handed over her phone, saying, "I've had similar thoughts. Henceforth, the leader of 4ASS shall be called Sophia von X. For ID—Sophia von Poison. Cool?"

Odette nodded as she jacked the phone into a tiny laptop, slightly larger than a box they found under the fountain. She erased the phone and downloaded new settings, "Awesome! Sophia it is."

Sophia had more questions she could ever answer. So many more... she dimmed the lights in hopes of getting some sleep before landing. She gazed out of the window for a while, watching the sea under the wings. Her mind jumped from event to event, trying to make sense of her chaotic journey. At last, sleep surrounded her: she drifted off into a dark dream.

The lights awoke the four women. Asha walked up the aisle. He touched Lifen's arm, "We're over Italy now, where Sophia indicated. The pilot is looking for a road that'll let us land and take off again."

Sophia stretched out her hands. She watched the Italian farmland rushing past under the aircraft. It was barely visible in the darkness. She felt at home, again.

Sophia frowned, "Are there any lights on this plane?"

"Not right now," Asha turned his face to answer. His eyes shined with hostility.

"Can planes just turn off their lights like that?"

"No," Asha smiled.

Sophia felt that he hated her but couldn't understand why.

The pilot's voice came over the intercom, "I've got a good stretch of sealed road. There are no cars. I'm touching down."

The dark ground beyond the windows swept up towards them. The craft shivered; tires screeched. The landing was abrupt. The plane trucked steadily to a halt. As soon as they were still, men in suits opened the stairs. The team of four trooped down with their gear and bags. Sophia held a very heavy satchel. She tried to keep it flat to avoid disturbing whatever was inside. All four stepped into the moist grass by the roadside. There were almost no lights, apart from the dull glow of the plane. A cold wind buffeted them. From behind the aircraft, which dominated the road, appeared a pair of headlights. It grew closer and closer...

CHAPTER 15

TRUTH, LIES, LEADERSHIP

"MERDE!" cursed Odette. "Who are they? What if they've seen the plane? What do we do?"

The car slowed, pulled over, and stopped. Their headlights washed over the bulk of the unlit plane.

"We can't let them leave and report seeing this plane, can we?" asked Sophia gravely, looking at Lifen for support.

Lifen shook her head, refusing to help. She needed to think.

"Asha, you and your men need to take whoever this is with you, and... make them disappear. Don't shoot them in the car, please. We'll be borrowing it. We want a clean car," Sophia ordered.

Asha looked at Lifen in disappointment, asking for permission, "Ms. Ong?"

"Yeah, it's necessary for all our sakes! Do as Sophia says."

Asha nodded. He made eye contact with one of his men. The two of them approached the car. A figure made indistinct by the bright backlighting, climbed out of the driver's side door and walked forward to meet them. Sophia saw how Asha pulled out his chromed gun. The figure quickly raised the arms. A second person climbed out of the car, cringing, held at gunpoint by Asha's companion. Asha marched the men over to the plane, past Sophia and the other women. When they stepped into the dull glow, provided by the plane's interior, Sophia saw an older man in a chequered shirt and a lad of about eighteen. Both looked scared and confused: the young man was crying, his lip trembling.

Sophia turned her face away: she didn't want to look at them. Asha marched them up onto the plane, saying, "The two of you are going to be our guests for a while. Don't worry, fellas, we have snacks."

The thick-necked brute that had bodyguarded them in the cabin was the only man left outside with the women.

"Any last orders, Ms. Ong?" he asked with no emotions.

"No, I'll be in touch." Lifen was glad to escape the so-called friends of her father.

"Are you guys going to kill them on the plane?" Madison blurted out.

The towering man adjusted his tie. "We're going to give them coffee and biscuits. After that, we'll tie a couple of rocks to their feet and drop them in the sea."

"Damn," murmured Odette, going pale.

The four women quickly ran to the car. It was a small yellow Peugeot in poor condition. They climbed in, fitting around the previous owners' baggage and rubbish. Sophia sat in the passenger seat, arranging the weight of the handbag on her lap.

In the meantime, Asha's men had loaded the bodies from the cargo hold onto the plane along with several large rocks from the roadside. No doubt, those rocks plowed out of the field years ago. Soon the air stairs retracted; the men were done on the Italian surface.

Sophia watched how the massive plane soared up into the sky. Without lights, it was almost invisible in the fog.

"Wake up! Where do we go now?" Odette asked, gripping the wheel.

It took them forty-five minutes to get to the small town called Segni, located on a hilltop in the Lepini Mountains. Sophia told the story about the incident near the bar, her peculiar savior, and his amazing sandwiches. The girls laughed; they enjoyed her company.

"We should ditch this car," said Sophia after a pause. "Leave it in there." She pointed into a public car park in front of a large building with a bulky ghastly sign of a plump boy, bowling a ball at skittles.

Soon, the four women were on foot, walking through a sprawl of suburban houses, sporadic hobby farms, and dark alleys. As the sun rose, they crossed the highway. Sophia turned to a familiar street and arrived at the GREEN BAR—Luca's place. It wasn't open. The front was still dark. They decided to wait at the back. When Luca opened the doors to the backyard of his bar, he raised his eyebrows—four delicious ladies sat in a row. He recognized one of them.

"Sabina?" he said. "I didn't think I'd see you back here so soon! Come on in! Who are your friends?"

Sophia walked into the bar, followed by her inner circle. Lifen eyed the short, bald, bearded man doubtfully, taking in the jumble of tattoos that festooned his arms.

"This is your guy?" she asked Sophia in a low voice.

Sophia answered, annoyed, "Just sit down and let us talk."

She was nervous. She couldn't bear the thought that her teammates were doubting her. Sophia joined Luca at the bar. Her friend seemed relaxed. He told her they could stay upstairs in one of the five rooms he'd recently renovated. He explained that the rooms are not fancy but clean and fresh.

Everything went surprisingly smoothly. Lifen paid for everything after she gained reassurance that her expenses would be reimbursed on payday. They all moved upstairs. The rooms were spartan, with small windows that overlooked the front of the bar. Odette cautioned Sophia about using any of her credit cards or for accessing money on it. Sophia cut them up, together with her old passport. *Now I'm a pauper. If I don't find a way to make money from that Turkish box, I will be a fugitive with no money to run with. I need to look inside. It could be filled with mold and dust,* she thought.

Sophia was alone in her room; the other three were downstairs. She took a shower and checked the place around her wound. It was gone. This never happened with her body before—she felt powerful, different, like the king of the world.

Well, no time like the present, she thought to herself. *I need to know what we've got here. There's no way I can sell it without seeing. Also, I have to think of how to find the man who hired Thomas...*Sophia placed the satchel on the bed, eased the heavy lead box out of it. She lifted it onto the bedside table, wiping its surface with a towel, to clean residue where necessary. On its lid, applied by some kind of stamp, were engraved the numbers 22:12, just like on the bronze tablet. The words from The Book of Revelation played nonstop in Sophia's head:

Look! I'm coming soon! My reward is with me,

And I will give to each person according to what they have done.

She tried to open the box. The lid would not budge. She drew the silver handled Hançer from her handbag, using its blade to break the seal. Sophia deformed the side, just enough to loosen the lid. When she felt the top move under her testing fingers, she paused. It took some time, but she gathered herself, trying to prepare for a big disappointment, unable to quell the nervous energy that filled her up, making her hands tremble. She lifted the lid. Inside was a layer of faded yellow fabric. Sophia moved it very carefully. Underneath was a large piece of vellum, subtly wrinkled, discolored from age, but still whole. She saw the words in black ink. The text was written in Hebrew. After careful examination, Sophia discerned—it was stiff, but not too fragile. She removed the pages from the box, one by one, each separated by a piece of cotton. She counted them all: the treasure contained only twelve pages. Each of them was covered in dense writing, free from illumination or embellishments, apart from the last page...it was slightly larger, edged in bizarre depictions of beasts. It seemed very different, even grotesque, from the other eleven. Down its center, she noticed a very odd Hebrew sign.

Sophia was an avid historian, a teacher of philosophy. She was familiar with Latin, Greek, and Hebrew, but struggled with the ancient usage of these complicated languages. She never encountered such old writings before. An hour later, she packed each page as she found them, back in the box. Then she sat in her chair, almost dead from swirling emotions. She knew the Christian world would be fascinated by this finding. Just imagine, the twelve lost pages from the Holy Bible... because, without a doubt, this is what it was.

. . .

Sophia left her room before lunch. The team decided to check the local shops for clothes and personal items. In the afternoon, they enjoyed oven cooked pizza, served by Luca himself. Sophia talked with Luca about the need to keep a low profile. She also asked him to call her "Sophia."

He smiled, "No problem, Sophia. Look, I can tell you're in some kind of trouble. Whatever it is, I don't think anyone's going to find you here. It's a lazy place—people don't get too curious."

That afternoon, Sophia decided she needed to know more about her companions if she was to command them with any grace at all. She decided to start with Lifen because the Asian lady truly fascinated her. She accompanied Lifen to her room and stayed for a drink.

The questions arrived from nowhere. "I'd like to know who those men that helped us at the airport are. How is it possible that you own private jets? It was wired to blackout the lights! If you're already a part of a criminal organization, I need to know, Lin."

Lifen looked up at the ceiling. She sighed, "No one else knows who I am. Even Thomas, our sweetheart, was just guessing. He thought I was a part of Yakuza."

"That might be so, but I'm your leader now. I drew the long straw...I want to know you."

"You're right, von X." Lifen sat on her bed, slowly pulling down her stockings. She undressed, wrapping her glowing body inside of the white bathrobe. "There's a massive holding company that spans UK and Asia. It owns hundreds of businesses and controls billions of dollars. One of its largest companies is Intercontinental Dairy Farmers—IDF. I know, doesn't sound dangerous. It imports and exports dairy products worldwide. It also stocks several major Asian and American brands." Lifen chuckled at Sophia's look of concentration.

This Sicilian chicken has no idea why I'm saying any of this, she thought to herself.

"I assume there's more to it than that…," Sophia encouraged Lifen to continue.

"My father is the CEO of IDF. He is a wealthy, powerful, and respectable man from Korea. Furthermore, our family is loyal. We all are very close: many of my brothers, sisters, aunts, uncles, nieces are in the company. I have an illegitimate brother, six years older than me. He is unknown to the public because he operates a shadow organization, which uses IDF's planes, money, and resources to act unseen or unsuspected. It avoids naming itself most of the time, but when it must, it calls itself The Red Syndicate. It also runs a global system of protection rackets. Do you know what I mean when I say that?"

Lifen dropped her bathrobe on the floor. She poured sweet almond oil inside of her palms, rubbed a small amount onto her belly, and spread a delicious-enough-to-eat smell in the room. She was so beautiful. Sophia wanted to help but was afraid to move. All of a sudden, Sophia's memories took her back to the history of the Sicilian Mafia. She recalled a story about the group of criminals, who offered physical and political protection to reputable organizations by attacking their enemies outside of the law or doing their dirty work. In return, they asked for money and favors. At the same time, both parts gained secrets and protection from the people they worked for.

"I know how protection rackets work," answered Sophia, watching Lifen's flexible body.

"I see, then I don't need to explain that The Red Syndicate does work for companies, criminals, and governments. Asha and his men helped us because they think I am heading with some special job for The Syndicate, which is a lie.

When my brother finds out, he'll reel me in, get me to do some boring work to repay him for my false play."

Sophia studied small Lifen's breasts, then coughed and asked: "Are you loyal to 4ASS or The Red Syndicate?"

"ASS Forever!" Lifen smiled. "If I wanted to be a permanent feature of The Syndicate, I'd already been doing it. I want my own life. I respect this team, Sophia. I'm admiring you. The money we could make is always a nice touch, too."

Sophia liked that Lifen didn't hesitate with her answer about loyalty. The last question was the hardest: "Does your father pay you, Lin?"

Asian beauty wrinkled her nose, "Yes, two hundred-thousand euros a month, but I want more. Who wouldn't?"

Lifen slowly crossed the room and opened the window. She bent half of her body over the edge, scaring Sophia to death. Sophia ran to the window, trying to pull her inside. Lifen turned, and then it happened, she kissed Sophia. It was a shy, innocent kiss. Sophia was stunned into silence. A look of despair came over Lifen's face.

"Do you want to leave?" she broke the silence.

A nervous pause had filled the air between the two women. Sophia swept her locks, revealing an expanse of tender skin across her neck. Lifen understood immediately. She touched the spot with her warm lips, nibbled on the soft skin, and whispered a message. Sophia couldn't resist anymore. She undressed, enjoying the attention of her new lover.

Later that night, Sophia talked to Madison and Odette. Madison Black was American and raised in southern Texas by an ex-military father who wanted a son. He was a doomsday prepper and ran a secret paramilitary organization made up of like-minded folks, who hoarded guns and trained for the collapse of society. They believed it was inevitable. Little Madison had been taught from a young age to prepare for the end times. She had been encouraged to be the roughest kind of tomboy. As a teen, she was known as a talented amateur kick-boxer, a skilled hunter, and a smart strategist.

Odette Donadieu-Poirot was French, poor, and an orphan. Her parents died when she was fourteen. Her foster family misunderstood her, that's why Odette turned to thievery—for distraction, fun, pocket money. She might be nothing but a common thief, but she got lucky. She befriended a professional burglar called White Fox. It happened when she, ironically ruined one of his heists by trying to rob the same gallery. They became lovers, then she became his second hand. When White Fox was arrested, Odette continued her risky life. She met Thomas von Essen in Paris, fell in love, and followed him every-where he went. She still couldn't believe he was dead.

CHAPTER 16

THE TWELFTH PAGE

THE NEXT SIX weeks turned into a blur for Sophia. She had expected them to be boring: hiding, waiting, researching, planning. But they were not. After examining everything she had taken from Thomas, Odette presented the bronze plate to the group along with the bad news that try-as-she-might, she could not crack his phone or gain access to his calls or notes.

"His phone is heavily encrypted. There's no way to get into it right now, not with the gear I've got, unless Lifen will buy me better equipment. So far, he has nothing else that gives us a clue about this plate or the box."

Sophia questioned her team about the perplexing interest to her birthmark. Madison confessed that Thomas had sent a photo to Papa Zen, the man who hired them.

"He didn't!" said Sophia incredulously.

"He did," replied Madison, enjoying the surprise on Sophia's face.

"Thomas wasn't a saint. By the way, we got offered an extra fifty grand to deliver you with the box."

Sophia was furious. How could she be so stupid? How

could she believe that Thomas was serious about their romance? She liked him a lot, she looked at him with admiration without the slightest idea as to what was in his heart. She wanted to be with him, surrounded by love that never really existed. She failed. Again. She probably should spend the rest of her life by writing satirical books about her relationships with men.

"So, you have no way of knowing who this Papa Zen is?" Sophia asked the group, waking up from her thoughts.

"Not really," explained Odette. "All we know is that he operates out of Jerusalem. He's rich and connected. He knew a lot about that box before we were involved, where to search the grave in Bingerbruck, and a fountain in Hagia. If you remember, he sent our team to Istanbul before the incident at the tomb. And the last, he knew something about your birthmark, too."

"I would like to meet him," said Sophia with a frown. "But I don't think I'm going to get the chance. The only way I can think of finding who this Papa Zen character is would be by questioning the organizers of the dig in Germany. They must know something about who sent Thomas."

"It's way too dangerous," said Odette. "We want to avoid the press, Interpol, and assassins that are looking for us. We still don't know why they wanted Thomas dead."

Odette shivered. She ran her hands up and down the goosebumps on her arms. The curtains were open. She looked down from the window at the bustling entrance of the GREEN BAR. She'd forgotten how it was—to be normal and free, to hang out with her friends, go to a wild party, and get lost with her lover. Hiding and sleepless nights became her new reality. She wished she could stop all that.

"It doesn't matter. Screw Papa Zen. I have another way of

selling this box and getting even more money," Sophia said slowly.

"How?" Lifen asked out of the corner. She drained her drink, straightened, and moved towards the next bottle. Sophia was worried about her. Almost ten days passed since their last conversation, and, strangely enough, they hadn't exchanged any word after that. It didn't make any sense. She felt blocked out.

"My brother is in the Sicilian Mafia. His boss might be interested." When Sophia said the last words, the girls exchanged hungry glances. "His Don is a religious and honorable man, in his own way. He'd love to own this box, and he's got plenty of money. It's simple...I'll contact my brother...he'll arrange the sale...we get paid."

"There's a ninety percent chance your brother's phone is tapped at the moment," Odette said nervously. She leaned to the wall, flicking the lights on and off.

"Really? Oh, I didn't think of it."

As Sophia wondered how she could reach her brother, Madison helped her out. "Maybe, you can call someone Interpol isn't going to think of and get them to tell your brother to get a new phone. You need to trust this person."

"Right! I can arrange that."

Sophia raised her chin. She was astonished by her own brevity and strength. She had never imagined she could talk like that. Her ego began to bloom.

Later that evening, she changed into pajamas, poured red wine in a glass, and opened a new version of the *Bible* from Hodder & Stoughton. Luca bought it on her request from the local bookshop. Sophia browsed the pages, swiftly moving to the

Book of Revelation. She found what she'd been looking for, and her face lit up, shining like Madonna's. She understood she was very close to solving the mystery of the twelve pages.

Before trying to arrange a sale, Sophia wanted herself and her partners in crime, if necessary, to have new identities. Odette said it would take a week to arrange. In the meantime, Sophia set herself to three tasks: an attentive study of the ancient Hebrew writings, training in hand-to-hand combat, and learning to shoot a gun.

Carefully photographing, translating, and examining old vellum was Sophia's meat and drink. During a week, she had completed an exhaustive translation of the first page, spending a great deal of time pondering the disturbing implications. She remembered that the letters of Paul were the earliest in the Christian literature, dating from around the mid-first century. The remaining books—the Gospels or Evangelion—were added later. If the four Gospels were compared with each other, a striking difference would emerge between John and the rest. Similarly, the Book of Revelation was attributed to John. Modern researchers insisted that it was a different John—an anonymous author, who used some kind of source from the Old Testament to create his prophecy, focusing on the second coming of Jesus. According to the Christian church, the aim of Revelation is to warn true believers and declare the plan of God. The Book was often served as a motivating factor in committing to follow Jesus' footsteps. So far, no one could ever crack an apocalyptic prophecy, because the last pages were stolen or lost. Sophia had no doubts, she held it in her hands— the sacred code to unlock the future of humanity.

The inscriptions on the twelfth page were a total mystery. Sophia believed that some signs had been taken from the Egyptian language but represented as if they were pictures of objects. The text was in ancient Greek, written in capital letters called *uncials*. She needed extra help from a competent archaeologist if she wanted to interpret it with essential respect to the Bible. The task was difficult but doable. Sophia decided to contact Dr. Pablo Gabriel Garcia, a famous biblical archaeologist and the Head of Egyptian Exploration College as soon as she got a chance.

Training, however, was unnatural to her. She didn't know where to start. She had always been the nerdy half of the Ferrara family. Time had changed—she wanted to be able to defend herself. Sophia thought of getting Madison to train her but instead opted to approach Luca. He was pleased and offered to tutor her personally. "There's nothing wrong with my self-defense classes, but you'll learn more quickly with one-on-one training," he explained, as he served Sophia her morning coffee. "How about we meet up at my gym at five-thirty this afternoon?"

Sophia trudged to the gym through a light rainfall. She was dressed in sweatpants and a singlet. She kept herself warm by a windbreaker she hugged around her. Luca's gym was an old run-down brick building next to a dilapidated garage. Inside, large mirrors lined the right-hand wall, free weights on metal wracks under them. Most of the floor was training mats. Two boxing bags hung from the roof on the far side of the enormous room.

Luca switched on the neon lights, locked the door, and said, "Let's talk goals, Sophia. What are you looking to achieve?"

Sophia knew exactly what she wanted. Cautiously, she answered, "There are most likely several dangerously trained men in my future. If they attack me, I want to be able to defend myself. I mean, I know what I'm asking is too much. It takes four to five years of hard training to become a black belt, right? In any case, I'd like to be as ready as I can."

Luca put his hands on his hips and shook his head. "No. Unlearn that. You want to win fights, right, not compete in martial arts or feel pride that you've mastered all the quirky moves of Wing Chun Kungfu? And if you want to win, then what you need to learn is surprisingly simple. It takes less time than you think, but it's not easy or pleasant."

Sophia was surprised. It sounded like Luca was telling her she could become a competent fighter quickly enough for it to be useful.

"How do we start? What's involved? How quickly do you expect I could improve?" Sophia looked both puzzled and suspicious.

Luca started slowly walking her over to the boxing bags. "I can tell you the three parts to your training in a nutshell. If you train with real focus, I can make it that each time you leave the gym, you could beat the version of you that stepped in."

Sophia sighed. She was ready to accept her new life as a fighter. Of course, she did miss calm Sundays with her family after the service at the La Martorana Church, but she believed it was her destiny now—to be a shepherd of 4ASS flock. Her job at the university was replaced with bouncy roads, her family life, with dead bodies. It was serious. It was real.

Luca stood on the mat and stretched his arms above his head. He cracked his knuckles and rolled his head side to side. After warming up, he tried to steal Sophia's attention again, "The first thing you need to know and what we'll focus on today is that the way to win a fight is to attack first. The second thing you need to know—never stop attacking as hard and as fast as you can. It's exhausting, Sophia. It's brutal. You need to learn how to hurt, disorient, and maul your opponent. It sounds like bad advice, but it's how you dominate a fight, especially if time is lacking or you are outnumbered. Always focus on neutralizing your enemy. Most martial artists do just fine in the dojo, but when they get in a real fight—they get hurt, scared—they find that all their carefully honed skills flee them. What I'm trying to say is that if you learn to fight calm, then you can't fight angry, scared, anxious...if you want to be able to fight in real situations, you need to learn to cooperate with your instincts."

"Oh, I don't know any basics. Where should I start?" asked Sophia, bewildered.

"Well, slowly and carefully, in a controlled environment. I piss you off, get into your head, then we train. It's hard work, because it's physical and psychological. It takes trust, too. You've got to remember, I'm your friend. I promise you this: if you train this way, I can make you dangerous in weeks, not years."

"I like the sound of that, Luca. I'm game!" Sophia decided to devote all her time to this training. The world of pleasures could wait. Lifen and the problems with the law could wait. She took a step forward, moving in slow motion, imitating the gestures she had seen in the action movies.

Luca shook his head hopelessly and complained, "Too early, I haven't finished yet. Part of becoming a great martial artist, or a big part of why it takes so long, is physical conditioning. If I punch a man in the teeth, it'll break the skin on my knuckles. If you do it, you could easily break the bones in your hand. I'll teach you how to strike and not hurt yourself. We'll use your knees, elbows, head."

"My head?" Sophia laughed.

It was impossible not to smile back when a Sicilian woman laughed. Her lips parted in a lovely way, freeing the sound of a thousand fireflies. She was so different from the women Luca had met before. She did everything with absurd, foolish passion. Sophia saw that Luca was under the impression of her smile. She touched his arm a little bit faster than usual, and it cooled his mind.

"It's tougher than you think. Do you remember when we met?" Luca interrupted the magic of the moment. He wasn't ready to fall in love.

Sophia nodded, recalling blood gushing from the thug's smashed nose.

"The head is a useful weapon if used right. If you are serious about being a dangerous fighter, then physical conditioning has to be part of your training. The stronger you are, the harder you hit. The harder you hit, the more mistakes you'll get away with," Luca continued, uneasy about the session.

"Okay, but I don't want to get muscular..."

"Don't worry. It's not that sort of muscle. I will advise your diet, give you some supplements to help things along," Luca suggested.

"What kind of diet? I can't live without my cannolis or granita," Sophia was more daunted by bland food and endless sauerkraut than hard work and sweat.

Luca smiled broadly, "There are two ways you can do it, either I can teach you how to diet and draw you up a plan, or you can eat the food I put in front of you, which is much easier. I promise you; it will be delicious."

"Sounds good. What's this going to cost, Luca?"

The man looked crestfallen. When he spoke again, his deep voice was much softer. "No need to pay me. The training is really hard. There'll be times you'll wish I was dead. It wouldn't be fair to charge you, girl."

Sophia studied his face, "Why are you doing this? Why are you so good to me?"

"You're in trouble, right? Big trouble?" asked Luca.

Sophia nodded.

"You came to me. You trusted me, Sophia. You've confided in me and turned to me to mentor you. I accept you as you are. Money doesn't matter; money would cheapen it."

"Thank you. You're a real friend, Luca," Sophia stepped close to him and gave him a quick, tight hug. "When do we start?"

"NOW!"

As the days marched by, Sophia lost track of the pain. She didn't know what hurt more—her mind or her body. Luca trained her as hard as she could handle. The first few days she was useless, unable to do anything, only cry or claw at him. Each time she tried to impress him, he pushed her further. She was a quick learner: she mastered punching, kicking, and driving her elbow into an opponent's face or throat. After training, she would work intensely on fitness and strength, tossing medicine balls until her hands hurt. Sometimes, Luca would poke her solar plexus, insult her, and push her around until she became angry and upset; then, they'd spar. It was horrible, but at the end of the first week, she knew how to channel her anger, how to cooperate with her instinct to flinch, how to duck and weave. She conditioned her hands by punching bags every day—although Luca said it would take years to develop solid bones. She trained seven days a week— five heavy workouts and two light—focused exclusively on technique or strategy. Sophia was exhausted. Despite that, she forced herself to find the time to learn how to shoot.

Luca told her about a new shooting club a half-hour drive away. It took two days to convince the owner to let them train after working hours. The owner of the club was reluctant and suspicious. He told them that his insurance wouldn't cover their gig after official hours, in case if anything awful would ever happen. It took a two-thousand dollar bribe, paid by Lifen, to make him hand over the keys three times a week.

Madison was the best gun woman on their team. In the first session, she didn't believe that Sophia had never shot before. She explained that amateurs would close their eyes and flinch, anticipating the retort of the gun. The untrained shooter missed ninety-nine percent of the time, but not Sophia.

"You don't flinch at all, which is good. Are you sure you've never shot before?" asked Madison.

"I haven't, despite my brother wanting to teach me. Why would I flinch when the gun is already in my hands? Thank God for that. I hate guns in other people's hands. They're so loud and deadly," Sophia joked.

As her time on the range passed, Sophia proved to be a talented shooter. She enjoyed the power of rifles but still struggled to maneuver with the gun in her hands. She was a little bit clumsy, even when she attempted to move swiftly and efficiently. Madison decided to focus only on those aspects.

Often, after training, Sophia felt like a sinner. Constant hiding, media news, and Thomas's absence reminded her that she was going against the fifth commandment—"Thou shall not kill." However, Sophia convinced herself that self-defense against an aggressor or threat is morally permitted. If there's no other solution, then you should do anything to protect yourself and those you love. *Killing that is based on love—how justified is it?*

Six weeks later, Odette invited the whole 4ASS gang to her room. The walls had pinups of complex diagrams and a sole printed picture of Francis of Assisi, with the words: *Start by doing what is necessary, then what is possible, and suddenly you are doing the impossible. For Odette from Baruch.*

Although Lifen, Madison, and Odette were mainly the same as they were six weeks ago, Sophia was transformed. She walked with an unusual spring in her step that she hadn't had since she was sixteen. Odette announced that she had some news. The good news was that neither she, Lifen, nor Madison were implicated in the Hagia incident, despite their arrival as a group in the right timeframe. It was probably a benefit of Istanbul being a tourist hotspot with so many foreigners flowing through its gates. The bad news was that Interpol and the Turkish government currently wanted Sophia. Worst of all, several fixes in the bounty hunting business had received word of a fifty-thousand dollar reward for her head.

"Can I move internationally if I'm hunted?" asked Sophia frowning.

"Well, you can. Your ID is solid. That will go a long way to protect you. I'd advise you to cut your hair and dye it to dark plum. When you see the photo on your new passport, you'll understand my suggestion," Odette explained.

"You managed to get her new ID onto government databases?" asked Madison.

"No. I'm not a magician or the CIA, Mad. It's identity theft. Her ID is that of a woman from Holland, called Maria Sophia von Poison, twenty-six-years old. Lucky us! She looks very similar to our boss. Check," Odette winked to Madison and handed the passport to perplexed Sophia. "You can always claim that you are using your middle name. The real Sophia, I suspect, has been sold into the white slave trade...just kidding. The look on your face was precious, Mad! Relax! Seriously, she is dead, and it's covered. My old buddy in Amsterdam helped me by not reporting her death. He also contacted his friends in Istanbul, who assisted him with moving Nina's and Thomas's bodies out of the country. Officially, they have never been there," Odette informed.

Sophia opened her new passport in awe. "She does look a lot like me."

"I've got you also a driver's license, birth certificate, an internationally accredited security, and bodyguarding license," Odette pointed to the screen of her laptop.

"Security and bodyguarding. Why?"

"To explain guns, silly. To justify them in certain circumstances. I hope it makes sense. Our job is very dangerous. 4ASS forever!" Odette howled at the end, like a wolf.

Lifen leaned on the wall. She was dressed in a long rose silk dress. She smoked, entertained by the conversation. At the end of Odette's speech, she tapped ash into the tray, then spoke, watching Sophia closely, "I'm not questioning your decisions, but the time has come to reach out to that Sicilian boss of yours, to see if we can sell what we have paid so dearly for. I know you've been examining the contents of that Hagia box. We've been quite patient, hoping you'd tell us when the time was right, what you had discovered. Or more to the point— how much it cost?"

Sophia nodded in agreement.

"I'll tell you what I know. I believe we have found the lost pages of the Bible. It is some kind of code for the Book of Revelation, describing the story of the new upcoming Messiah. It doesn't line up with the Bible we know. It adds a new perspective on how the world ends, that changes everything..." The three women stared at her, a quirky smile starting to grow on Lifen's lips.

"Oh my God," interrupted Madison. "That's got to be worth a fortune, girls! I can't believe it is still in one piece!"

"It is hard to believe," doubts fleeted across Sophia's face. "I think it was placed there much later, probably in the fifth century, maybe when the last from Jesus's tribe were moved, killed, or buried. Someone also added the bronze plate to the tomb in Germany. Very strange! I say it suggests the existence of a conspiracy or secret society. Maybe Papa Zen is the answer to all our questions?"

Lifen raised her eyes from the phone, insisting, "Whatever it is... we need to sell it. Let's focus on that! Is our best bet still the Sicilian Mafia?"

"Before we do, I have to say," interjected Sophia, "I don't think Papa Zen wanted the whole scripture. I think he wanted only the twelfth page. The twelfth page is the answer to everything!"

CHAPTER 17

DOCTOR GARCIA AND THE LEFT EYE OF HORUS

THE GREATEST OF all mysteries is the origin of mankind. Throughout the ages, people have speculated about the first human creation, regarding it as unique, a gift from God. After all, he created man in his own image...

These simple words from the Book of Genesis made known to the world the truth of the first humans' origins. God's words had the virtue of simplicity—in the image of God, male and female, he created them.

The prophet Moses was one of the first to spread word of God's power. He spoke as divine authority, declaring the Lord's beautiful message to his flock, his important creation. Ever since, no one has contradicted Israel's great leader. His proclamation was the axiom. But what if the truth had another source? What if the Egyptian Gods and Goddesses had paved the way for creation? The precise wording, delivered by Moses, has been written and taught throughout generations, until now. Facts about the birth and death of humanity, which have been concealed in Egyptian symbols and buried under the fountain in Hagia, have finally been revealed. All Sophia had to do was bring it to light, understand the message, and expose it to the public. She was aware of the obstacles. The translation required specialized knowledge, or at least, professional advice. The Egyptian symbol in the middle reminded her of a bird, perhaps, Horus. Sophia sensed that the artifact was authentic. The lost pages from heaven were harmoniously linked with each other, but she did not know how.

The greatest of all mysteries of mankind is how it ends... imagine God has a complete plan for the human race, for every person who ever lived or ever will. Imagine that you have access to that plan, but you cannot fully understand it.

Sophia sighed. With a heavy heart, she opened her phone and sent a message to Dr. Garcia, the Head of Egyptian Exploration College, attaching a photo with the short text from the twelfth page. Almost immediately, her phone rang. The following conversation took place:

Dr. Garcia: Let them cut down the head and let them destroy it. The next day, when the earth grows dark, and the heart of Horus falls to the ground, I shalt come to life again.

Sophia: Hello! Doctor Garcia? I don't understand.

Dr. Garcia: Forgive me, I'll explain in a second. Good afternoon, Sophia. I'm thrilled you have contacted me. The information you have provided is sensational! It will blow the minds of all believers and non-believers around the globe. Everything I just said was the translation of the text you sent me.

Sophia: So, I was right? The text has something to do with the Egyptian gods.

Dr. Garcia: Considering the sign of the udjat-eye, also known as the eye of Re or Horus, I believe you are on the right path to crack the message. And I'd like to help! Please, call me Pablo.

Sophia: Thank you, Pablo, I appreciate it. I need help with reading the Egyptian symbols. They're rich with meanings and associations. I lack the necessary knowledge, you see.

Dr. Garcia: Right. About that... I heard Interpol is looking for your 4-ASS group. I don't want to get involved in criminal activities, but the piece you've got is truly precious. I'd like to help, Ms. Ferrara.

Sophia: I'm glad to hear that. You can call me Sophia. What do you personally think about that mystical verse?

Dr. Garcia: I think, as an old member of The Left Eye of Horus Society, it says that the one from Christ's family has to go through some kind of purification. For example, in the photo you sent to me, Horus's eye is surrounded by germs. It's an illness which is threatening humanity or earth.

Sophia: I don't understand. Do you mean the last descendant of Christ's family has to die?

Dr. Garcia: Almost. A near-death experience would be good enough. First, we have to translate the accompanying texts and signs; second, we have to find him or her...

Sophia: If only it could be that easy.

Dr. Garcia: I'm in Spain right now.

Sophia: Aren't you scared to meet Sophia von X in person? You said you didn't want any trouble with the police.

Dr. Garcia: Well, I hope we can make a deal.

Sophia: A deal?

Dr. Garcia: I will help you with the full translation...

Sophia: And in return?

Dr. Garcia: You'll let me keep at least one page.

Sophia: You are crazy! By the way, do you have any friends or members of your Left Eye Society in Israel?

Dr. Garcia: I do. Why?

Sophia: I think it's best if we arrange our meeting there, Pablo. I'll let you know the details.

CHAPTER 18

THE PRICE OF REVENGE

THE NEXT MORNING, at six, Sophia was already at the door of Luca's gym. She planned to contact her brother today, to arrange a delicate exchange that would make or break the newly formed 4ASS. She needed to burn off some nervous energy before she made that call. Luca was already there, alone. The two of them warmed up, chatting about the training strategy. Luca tried to put off Sophia's concentration by getting blows past her guard, which was getting increasingly difficult.

After two hours of hard training, while unlacing Sophia's boxing gloves, Luca said, "There's that look again. You smile at me, then look down. I always think I've done something wrong."

"It's nothing, forget."

"It can't be nothing. Can I know?"

"It's not your fault. I just don't like...beards."

Luca looked a little insulted. He was very proud of his beard.

"I know! It's silly. My ex-husband had a beard, and he was...he was abusive. He only hit me twice, but he lied and manipulated his way out of it," anger crept onto the attractive features of the Sicilian woman. "As you can see, I've developed this aversion to beards. I'm working on it!"

Sophia looked to the side, not wanting to see Luca's face right now. Luca stayed quiet but didn't seem angry. He got Sophia to unlace his gloves and left for the showers to freshen up. Sophia followed. The showers were three private cubicles in one big room. Sophia soaked in hot water, mostly worrying about the sale of the Hagia box. Her brother would have to do the negotiations with his superiors. It wasn't so easy. Does he have what it takes to broker a multi-million-dollar trade? Whose side would he favor? Her head was still humming with these thoughts when she stepped out of the shower to public space, only to find the unknown man with a towel around his waist, shaving in front of the mirror. It took her a moment to realize it was Luca. He looked so different without a beard. He wiped his face and turned to grin at her.

"How do I look now?" he asked, his grin looking bigger and his head somehow smaller without his beard.

"Luca! Why did you do that?" Sophia asked, regret clouded her face.

"It's best to shave just after a hot shower, bec...,"

"Did you do that because of me? Because of what I just said?"

"You were uncomfortable."

"I shouldn't get to decide what haircut you have, Luca!"

"True. You didn't, not once in the last six weeks. I should be able to choose my cut, and I prefer the one you're comfortable with," he explained.

Sophia walked over and kissed him on the cheek. "You're too good to me."

"I don't think so. I think the other men in your life have

not treated you well enough. That's all." Luca paused, looked in the mirror, and added, "Bald from two ends, what a day!"

Sophia sat on her bed with a notebook opened next to her. She looked down at jotted information and names. She decided to call Ucko Lifebelt, a new assistant at the university. He had given her his number if she ever wanted any help or to resign from her job. She was assured that Ucko would never call the authorities—he hated the government.

Ucko already knew. He'd seen her face on the news. A photo that made her look short and stupid had been broadcasted worldwide. The first thing he said was that he was convinced she was framed, so convinced she didn't need to explain anything. He also happily agreed to carry her message to Matteo.

Matteo's call came sooner than Sophia had expected. When she picked up, he spoke immediately. "Thank God, you're alright! Dad is furious. What on earth happened?"

"That's a long story, Matti. Tell Dad I'm all right. I'm sorry I didn't call you earlier. I had to lay low. I'm sure you understand. Also, I have reasons I've called you, aside from my safety."

"We've had the authorities visiting and asking about you, seeking your whereabouts. FBI, Interpol, police, some weird thugs, all kinds of groups. We've told them nothing, except that you're on holiday and we have no idea where you are. Mom is devastated, I'm afraid. How could she not be? She doesn't think you're involved...My take on it, however, is that...did you really do this? I mean the Hagia robbery," Matteo asked with concern.

"I don't know what I did. I don't know why I did it, but

yes, I got involved in something. There is no way out. Anyway, every cloud has a silver lining. That's one of the reasons I've called you Matti."

"You've got my attention, sis."

"As you know, I'm being accused of stealing an artifact. I've had time to carefully examine what I've got: it's proven to be some rare religious writing. If I told you how old they were, or who wrote them, I wonder if you would believe me, but remember I'm an avid historian and trained philosopher."

Matteo could hear her breathing through the phone.

"Are you trying to sell stolen manuscripts to the Mafia?" he asked.

"That's right."

"What's happened to you? I hear it is you, your voice, but I would never have guessed you capable of this, Sabina."

"It's been a rollercoaster ride. It makes a bit more sense when you hear the whole story. Maybe one day I'll have the time to tell you."

"Are you ever coming back? Are you coming back to a normal life? To be honest, after creating ASS-something, I can't even think of how you could. What a crazy name for a criminal group..."

"I'm afraid not, Matti. I suppose I'm a bit like you, only more of an outsider."

"It must be in the blood," her brother joked, but there was little humor in his voice. "I can't help you sell this manuscript unless you tell me what it is. You've said I might not believe you, but you've got to tell me sometime, and it might as well be now."

Sophia hesitated. The knowledge was too dangerous. She decided to give him something, a half-truth. A half-truth is not a complete lie; it's only some way concealed, covered facts.

She said, "In brief, I have uncovered the original writing that I believed to be the lost pages of the Bible. The code of Revelation. The evidence is overwhelming!"

There was a long pause on the other end of the line, then Matteo spoke softly, "Are you serious?"

"I am."

"I have to agree: our Don would be interested in those writings."

"Of course, he would be!" Sophia searched for the right words to say but couldn't find any.

"It's going to take me some time. Understand, the Don's going to want his experts to verify this finding. He's not going to pay good money or take the risk on your word alone."

"What stops him from simply taking the manuscript once it's in the hands of his experts? Can he be trusted?"

"He's not that kind of man, sis. You'd have to be crazy to spill blood while acquiring the word of God; it sounds like bad luck. We can arrange it so that you can have some of your people present when the manuscripts are being examined. If you have people...I'm not sure how safe or supported you are."

"Safe enough, and I have people. I just don't want this to backfire. I want everyone to get what they want: you, me, the Don."

"Alright. I'll start negotiations. Can I contact you on this number?"

"Yes. Make certain that no one taps that phone. Don't call anyone else with it...," Sophia tried to coach her brother. She heard how he sucked a breath in through his teeth.

"I do have burners. It is the twenty-first century," Matteo snorted.

"One more thing. Do you remember before I went on holiday, you spoke to me about wanting to make Dario pay for the things he's done to me?"

"How could I forget?" her brother answered, raising his voice.

"I've been thinking about it," Sophia paused as her mind wandered to the kindness and empathy Dario had shown her when she had just met him. "I've decided that maybe I haven't seen things clearly. I'll leave what happens to him in your hands."

Matteo smiled, "You've made the right decision. I'll contact you soon, Sabina. Love you."

"I love you, too."

Matteo slid his phone into his pocket. For some reason, he wasn't worried about his 'little' sister. He had heard the steel in her voice; it sounded like she had found herself. She had finally gotten Dario's claws out of her flesh! Overall, ironically, Matteo felt more comfortable about his sister's well-being now than he had when she left so troubled and lost on her holiday.

The gorgeous leader of 4ASS sat and pondered. The conversation with Matteo had gone well. She had expected him to be angry and condescending, but he'd taken her seriously. She was anxious for his next call.

Sophia walked downstairs to the bar. She found her companions eating a cold lunch: salami, cheese, bread, and beer. She joined them, reporting about the chat with her brother.

"I suppose we play the waiting game," said Lifen. She glanced at her gold watch and rushed to the door.

"In a hurry?" Sophia tried to stop her. She grabbed Lifen's arm, exploding with a hearty weird laugh. Sophia knew she'd made a fool of herself, running after a luxury, sexual thrill. She felt embarrassed by the unknown erotic thirst, creeping horror of forbidden pleasures, and the night she spent in Lifen's room. At the same time, all she ever wanted was to be invited there *every damn night.*

"I don't like the noise. See you tomorrow, girls. Asha is waiting outside," Lifen answered, waving goodbye.

Sophia felt the strange urge to grip her empty glass and throw it to the back of the well-dressed Asian. Was that desperation, the frustration of the past six weeks, or the desire to feel loved? Sophia couldn't tell.

———

Matteo couldn't believe his luck: he was finally going to get to teach Dario—that fat sack of shit—a lesson. *There's no time like the present*, he thought to himself, while studying his reflection in the mirror. *I might as well get it over and done with. This is years overdue. If I leave it hanging, it will no doubt distract me. I'm going to need all my wits for that negotiation with the Don.*

He tried not to think about the delicate affair he was about to get embroiled in, negotiating the sale of a stolen treasure with the Don of the Sicilian Mafia while being watched by international authorities, because his sister—the very broker of the treasure—had managed to commit a crime so hair-raising that it had garnered worldwide attention. Matteo slipped a .38 automatic into the back of his belt. He also slid a flick knife into his pocket, making a note of the second knife that he had strapped to his ankle. To be honest, he didn't think he would need any of these things. Dario was plump and lazy. He had never given Matteo the impression of someone who knew how to fight. Dario, in his eyes, was a man of cruel words, a manipulative bastard with a permanent sneer, but that wouldn't help him tonight.

Matteo was happy. His victim was only a twenty-minute drive away, at home or the nearby bar. As far as Matteo knew, Sophia's ex had no job. Instead, he was lounging around the house that his wife had let him take.

Matteo trotted downstairs into the garage and stepped into his BMW. Soon, he was cruising through the streets of old Palermo. Thinking about Dario had put Matteo's soul in the perfect mood to visit him. His jaw, mind, and fist were set. He pulled up at the two-story home where, for so many years, his sister had lived. He recalled that the gardens and yard were always so beautiful and immaculate. Now they were overgrown; the house looked almost abandoned. Matteo was halfway up the garden path when he noted a small security camera (he was certain he had not seen it before), gazing down from the eaves. It seemed that Dario had grown more cautious with time; maybe he had other enemies, too. If so, Matteo would certainly like to meet them; they could trade notes. He wondered if Dario, having seen him coming, would pretend he wasn't home.

He walked up to the door and, ignoring the doorbell, knocked loudly. A minute later, the door opened. It was Dario, wearing dirty sweatpants. He was taller than Matteo, with a long bushy brown beard. Dario stepped aside, inviting him in, "Come in, Matteo. I certainly wasn't expecting to see you here."

"Why not? We're family, aren't we?"

"Sure. What is this all about?" Dario closed the door. "Is

this about the trouble Sabina's managed to get herself in? What do you know about it?"

Matteo pondered whether he should drive his fist into Dario's fat belly right here in the hall or wait until they moved to the living room, where it was less likely to be overheard. When Matteo didn't answer, Dario walked down the hall into the living room, over to the alcohol cabinet, where he took out two glasses. He poured himself a shot of whiskey, looking over at Matteo with a question.

"Scotch, on the rocks," said Matteo.

Dario walked into the kitchen to get two pieces of ice. He sloshed scotch on them and carried the drink out, to his ex-brother-in-law.

"You're not here about Sabina, are you?" asked Dario as he sipped his whiskey.

"No. I'm not here to talk about where Sabina is or what she's doing. As a matter of fact, I have no idea where she is."

Dario refused to play along. He picked up the knife for ice, tapped it against the table. Matteo followed each of his moves.

"Why are you here? Did you finally want to look at some of my photography? I've been doing very cool work with drones lately..." The beginnings of a sneer played around Dario's lips.

The conversation was starting to annoy Matteo. He flung his drink in Dario's face. Dario screwed up his eyes, stumbling back with a cry of surprise. Matteo stepped forward, drove his fist as hard as he could into the victim's ribs. He was genuinely astonished at how little effect it had. The young mafioso had expected that Dario would hit the floor like a sack of potatoes, but instead, his strong fist found solid muscle. Dario wiped his eyes, poured one more glass, and grinned broadly, "Finally taking the initiative, Matteo? Well done. Have you decided you should take things into your own hands even though your sister begged you not to touch me?"

"You'll be pleased to know she gave me full permission," spat Matteo, full of wrath.

Dario's smile faded a little. "Did she now? Bad girl. You know, I'll have to talk to her about that decision."

"I think you'll find her surprisingly hard to locate."

"We'll see. After all, I know her better than you do."

Matteo growled and jumped at Dario, this time punching his throat. Dario's jab knocked aside. Matteo smiled and continued: he punched Dario's face, ribs, an uppercut to the jaw. But each time Dario drove the blow aside with his big forearms. Despite what he'd believed, Matteo quickly realized that Sabina's ex could fight: he was much stronger than he looked. Determined to finish it, Matteo stepped nimbly aside and drove a punch into his gut. Rather than defend himself, the man with a bushy beard absorbed the blow and swung a roundhouse of his own. Matteo ducked. He swung two punches at Dario's head and failed.

The next punch from Dario knocked the wind out of him. Staggering, he brought up his arms, trying to stop the next sledgehammer blow from Sabina's ex, but it broke through his guard.

"Having fun yet?" sneered Dario. "Is it everything you hoped it would be, shithead?"

Matteo didn't answer. He wiped the blood from his lips, pulled out his flick knife, and snapped out the blade. He sprang forward and slashed it at Dario's torso. Dario stepped back, fended the blade aside, but imperfectly, the blade cut his flesh. Blood began to dribble down his forearm. With a roar, Dario kicked at Matteo, who didn't anticipate the attack. Dario's boot caught him in the stomach.

Sabina's brother felt his ribs bend as he was hurled back into a chair. For a moment, he shuddered, unable to breathe, then slowly, agonizingly forced himself to rise... He froze. Dario was pointing a pistol at him.

"Fight not going well enough for you?" panted Matteo.

"I needed to pull mine before you pulled yours, Big brooother Ferrara!" the host of the house looked like a wacky monster.

"You wouldn't dare, bitch. Your neighbors will hear the gunshots. How do you think you'd fare in prison?"

"I'm not so certain anyone will hear the gunshots, little dummy. This house is surprisingly soundproof. I should know; I'm the one who soundproofed it." Dario went to the far side of the room, screaming like a Tarzan.

"You know who I am? You know who I'm associated with?" muttered Matteo, starting to get his breath back. "If I go missing, our Don will come looking around. You won't get away with this."

Dario grinned, clapping his hands, "You know, I'm glad we're having this conversation. All these fuckin' years together, as a family union, and we've shared so few words. I really must talk with Sabina. She's not amusing anymore. Why don't you tell me where she is? I might let you live."

"She's not your plaything, you fat piece of shit!"

"I suppose we'll put your little theory to the test. Let's see how good your friends are at getting revenge! Ready?" asked Dario, grimacing.

Without any warning, Matteo pushed out of the chair and lunged sideways. His hand slid back for his gun. Dario's pistol went off. Matteo felt pain lance through his body as it bit into his side, ripping flesh. The blood gushed on his suit, and he collapsed on the floor. His vision was blurred, his limbs shook, but by sheer focus, he managed to force his arm to move, aiming his gun at Dario. He couldn't see him but fired anyway. That shot buried the bullet in the wall. Dario couldn't stop. His next bullet tore into Matteo's ribs, puncturing both of his lungs.

The whole body of Matteo Ferrara was consumed by pain. His vision went red, black, white—he slumped lifeless into a pool of his blood.

———

Dario examined his arm. The cut was shallow. He picked up his drink and slowly finished it. He was delighted with the pool of sticky blood, creeping across the carpet. He wouldn't bother cleaning it. He'd leave it here for the mafia to find. He hoped the body would be rotting by that point.

Dario had grown tired of lingering here at home, waiting for Sabina to crawl back to him. It seemed that bitch had no intention to come back. *That's fine. I'd like to see what kind of tune she'd play face-to-face with me.* Sabina's ex-husband thought to himself. He checked Matteo's pockets and started packing his bag. The international authorities might not be able to find his wife, but he knew he could.

C H A P T E R 19

L O V E , D E A T H , M O N E Y

S O P H I A H A D E X P E C T E D Matteo to call back in the next few days, but a fortnight dragged past without any contact. She wasn't worried at first, but after three days, she became increasingly agitated. She distracted herself with training, convincing her mind that Matteo was busy with complex negotiations, finding experts, arranging the place to examine the script.

Eventually, Sophia caved in and called Matteo's number, wondering if his burner phone still existed. It picked up almost immediately. A wave of relief washed through her. She exclaimed, "Matti, thank goodness! You haven't contacted me for five days. How's everything going?"

The voice that answered did not belong to her brother. It was the cold voice of Dario, her ex-husband, "I'm afraid Matti is not here right now."

Sophia felt her blood chill in her veins.

"Oh my God! Dario? How do you have this phone? Where's Matteo? What's going on? Have you done something to him?!?" Sophia couldn't keep the panic out of her voice.

"Such accusations!" Dario laughed, "Why would I do anything to your brother, Love? We are one family."

"Speak straight with me, Dario! For once in your life! Tell me what's going on!"

"When am I ever dishonest? I have no reason to hurt your brother, unless, of course, he came to my house and tried to hurt me...unless, of course, he came to my house with a fuckin' gun. Ah, but why would he do that, Darling?"

Sophia sat in silence—her body trembling. Something horrible had happened. It was her fault Matteo had gone to Dario's house. She should have said nothing.

Sophia growled, "Tell me what you've done. Is he still alive?"

"I don't need to tell you anything. Why should I tell you? You're the one who sent him. Aren't you? You sent him to kill me, bitch! When I find you, I'll make you beg," toxic phrases quickly escaped his mouth. At that moment, Dario showed his real nature.

"He wasn't going to kill you! He was just angry at you. Angry for the things you've done to me, to the Ferrara name. Where is he? Please...Why do you have his phone?" the woman sobbed. She waited for the spasms in her heart to slow down. She sat on the floor, pulled her knees up to her chin, and hugged them. She didn't move for a few seconds.

"As always, you're soooo full of curiosity," mocked her ex-husband.

"What is wrong with you? I didn't think you were this much of a psycho!"

"Maybe you should have gotten to know your husband better, Darling, rather than stonewalling me and spending all your free time at work."

"I'm not starting this again, okay?" Sophia could feel irrational panic gripping at her. "Tell me where he is, tell me what you've done! I hate you!"

"See you soon, Love. Bye."

Sophia could not believe what had just happened. The phone was dead. He'd hung up on her. There was no point calling back. She knew something had happened to her little brother, but she had no way of discovering what. She needed to talk to her girls.

Fifteen minutes later, all four members of 4ASS were drawn together in Sophia's room. She was unable to hold back her tears when she told them about the horrible call.

"We're not that far away from Sicily," said Madison. "We should pay him a quick visit."

"We can't afford to do that," Lifen replied. "It's far too dangerous. He could easily be watched. Any of her family could be watched."

"I know this sounds odd," said Odette softly. "But don't you think he was trying to keep you on the phone? You had a very long conversation with him, mocking and cajoling you. I understand you are trying to find out what happened to Matteo, but what if your ex had tracked your location?"

"How would he be able to do that?" asked Sophia. "He's not that technical."

"Are you sure that he couldn't have traced a phone call? Odette could. Five-year-old kids can!" Lifen grimaced.

"He likes computer games, writing, pornography. He often locks himself in his study. Lately, he spent days with his new photo camera. He often drives to different parts of Italy to take pictures," Sophia shook her head. "I think he's a more artistic person than technical."

"Typical Ripper behavior," whispered Madison. Sophia didn't hear her. She examined the old list of her contacts on the phone, trying to find a quick solution to the problem—locating her brother.

Lifen took out a new mini-pad from her bag and jumped directly to business. "Alright. Next question... we need to decide how on earth we're going to sell an artifact. Do we try to make contact with the Sicilian Mafia again? Do you think you would still have leverage with your brother missing?"

Sophia looked at the Asian beauty in shock. She said in a cold voice, "I'm much more concerned in finding out what happened to my brother than what angle to take in selling the manuscript."

"She's got such awful news, Lin," said Odette, calming both sides. "You can't expect her simply to forget that."

"I don't expect anyone to forget anything," Lifen answered, exasperated. "But we have to remain professional. You're our leader, Sophia. We're relying on you. We need money from this sale to become free and mobile."

"You're a cold fish, Lifen, but you're right. Everything that you're saying is true. It's just my heart is being eaten alive without knowing what happened to my Matti," Sophia started to cry.

Madison couldn't bear it. She proposed to investigate the situation in discretion: to hire private detectives, who don't know who's hiring them; ask them to poke around and email the information they'd found. Odette agreed. She said it would cost them only a couple thousand dollars, and Sophia's heart would be at peace. Lifen promised to contact the investigating company through Asha.

"As for making a deal, I'm not confident in brokering a sale to the Mafia without Matteo. They don't know me. They've got little incentive to give a group as small as ours a fair deal. Plus, I'm a wanted criminal, so they've got blackmail and leverage over me." Sophia explained her view about selling the artifact to the Ndrangheta family.

"Any backup plan? We can't live in the GREEN BAR forever," Lifen sighed. "I don't dare to use any of my father's contacts. Not now. Maybe we should try to locate private collectors, those we can negotiate with."

"I'll get on to that," Odette's face lit up. "I'll need a couple of days."

"If that doesn't come up with anything," Sophia rounded up the meeting, "I'll try to reconnect with the Ndrangheta and arrange a negotiation by myself."

"Do you think we should stay here, Sophia? Maybe it's time to change the nest?" Madison was bored in the sleepy Segni. Her hands and soul desired new actions. Odette disagreed. She voted for staying in one place. The town was tranquil, friendly, cheap. Sophia was unsure if it was a good idea to leave. She couldn't believe Dario could trace her phone call. No way he had been keeping her on the line to find out where she was. He was simply cruel and manipulative, as always.

"Let's stay here. We'll change the nest as soon as we find the buyers," Sophia decided.

———

Dario unplugged the mobile from his laptop, turning both off. He packed it in his travel bag, which he placed on the low bedside table. It wasn't his bedside table. It belonged to Gianna.

Until ten days ago, he'd lived in Palermo, but now he was in Rome. The first thing Dario did after leaving his house was call an old army friend, Roger Weber. Roger lived in Constance, a small city located in the South of Germany. After the army, he worked at the border booth, placed on the A11-highway, between Switzerland and Germany. He was a divorced drunk gambler with severe post-traumatic syndrome. His two kids lived with their mother, and Roger met them only on weekends. Dario always suspected that Sabina took off to visit the newly discovered holy tomb. She was always crazy about caves, archaeological finding, and Jesus. He contacted Roger immediately, back in January, asking for help to locate his run-away-wife. It was easy then. Unfortunately, after one more drunk incident, Roger had been fired. This time, Dario was on his own.

The last report from Roger had stated that Sabina's purple Peugeot was still based in Frankfurt. Dario knew Sabina would never abandon 'Holmes.' He checked the car on the day of his arrival in Germany. He noticed how long 'Holmes' had sat in the locker and decided to get back to Italy—to wait for when his wife called Matteo's phone...Finally, the wait was over. He was delighted to find she was only an hour's drive away. It wouldn't take long for him to get to her new location and set up surveillance. He should pay Gianna one last visit. After all, she had been so kind to him, letting him sleep in her house, free of charge. Gianna was in the basement of her house, chained to the boiler.

They met in a bar. When his attempts to seduce her failed, he pretended to be embarrassed. It worked before; it worked now. He said that he had nowhere to stay and offered her one-thousand dollars to sleep on her couch for a couple of days until he could get in contact with an old friend. The poor girl, foolishly, had agreed. He'd had his fun with her, only giving her water and food after she had answered exhaustive questions about her sex life, friends, and family. He made her believe that she had been carefully chosen, that this was all about her. It was a lie. He promised that he had no intention of doing anything wrong, but he had speculated that, at some point, if he wanted a *pet*, then it will be very easy to crawl back into her life and terrify her. Information is the key! Thinking about it made him smile. Yes, he would like to use pretty, scared Gianna for his dirty role-plays, but only after he had finished his business with Sabina.

———

Sophia did not normally drink to excess. She'd tried it when she was a teenager, but she didn't like the lack of control, vomiting, and worse, feeling wretchedly sick in the morning. Today was different. Haunted by not knowing what had happened to Matteo, having heard Dario's voice again, with everything thrown into uncertainty, she felt a pressing need to turn to the bottle. Luca didn't mind helping. He filled her glass anytime it was empty. He was curious what had perturbed the girls so much and figured, if Sophia got drunk, maybe she'd confide in him a little more than she had in the past. The last days, all he did was dream about having sex with her.

Odette sat with a tipsy Sophia in the corner of the room, listening to the horrors of her relationship with Dario. A man shuffled in the door and doffed his hat. He was a regular by the name of Sergio—a retired farmer, truly comic personality, who sometimes made coin imitating bird calls. He approached Luca, speaking in Italian, "My friend, you told me to mention if anyone came around asking about your lovely guests. As a matter of fact, somebody has. As you know, my daughter works at The Galloping Horse hotel... She told me somebody asked for a woman called Sabina, showing a photo of your friend over there. My daughter said she didn't like the look of that guy. Don't worry, she didn't tell him anything, but I don't know who else he's been asking. I came right here as soon as she called me...not late?"

"Thanks, Sergio. You are a good man. This one's on the house," Luca signalled one of the serving lads to take his place. He quickly walked over to Sophia's table. Leaning in close, he said in a low voice, "Bad news, girl. Someone's in town looking for you. The man was asking after you at the hotel, up on the highway. He used your old name. Do you think it is the FBI agent?"

Sophia stared at him for a moment, then looked at Odette with a dumb question in her eyes.

"We need to get the news to others and get out of here," Odette said in a rush, wide-eyed. Both women rose. Odette immediately ran upstairs, knocking on the doors.

Sophia hesitated, looking at Luca, "I've got to leave, Luca, I'm sorry. I don't know when I'll be back."

"I knew this day would come. Run. Don't think about me. If anyone comes in here asking, I'll send them in the wrong direction."

Sophia hurried upstairs to her room. She stuffed all her possessions, including the artifact box, in the bag. At that moment, Sophia received a text from Odette: *I am in the local park. Had sprung a getaway car. Look for a white panel van on the far side.*

Sophia quickly forwarded the text to the rest of the team. She hurried downstairs, stopping at the bustling bar, to see if any new faces had emerged. When Luca gave her the nod, she went out of the backdoor.

Outside, she put on a shoulder holster and sheathed the Magnum pistol that Madison had given her. She also pushed her second gun, a Glock 17, into the back of her belt. She dropped some loose ammunition into each pocket, ready for a new fight.

Sophia stayed alert, hoping not to see strange dark figures stepping out of a car or levelling a gun on her. She hurried along the grim facade of the Chiesa di S. Pietro, down the alley-way, in which she and Luca had first talked, emerging into the isolated small park, cluttered with cars of visitors and business owners. Looking on all sides, trying to see if anyone was following her, Sophia ran through the cars, searching for a white panel van.

———

Dario sat in his hotel room. He was in the same rural town as Sabina. During the day, as disguised as he could manage, he'd placed small cameras around the bar she was staying at, under gutters, between bins. So far, none of them had been found. Dario enjoyed the conveniences of the twenty-first century. Small observation devices, once only available to spies, could easily be ordered through mail for home security and personal use.

He had seen his ex-wife come and go during the day. He had once noticed how she walked into the bar with a young woman that he assumed was one of her partners in crime. He wondered how she was so relaxed with an international price on her head.

Today, after sunset, he saw her hurrying out of the backdoor of the GREEN BAR, pale-faced, carrying bags. His Sabina was obviously scared, preparing to move on. Dario packed his things by throwing them in his car. He loved the rush of the chase.

———

Sophia spotted the white panel van. She approached it quietly, looked around, and slid the door. Odette was sitting inside, "Madison will be here any minute. She's not bothering to go back to her room. Lifen is still there. I don't like that she's alone, but it should be okay. They're looking for you, not her."

Not long after, Madison and Lifen arrived from different directions at the same time.

"Quick! Get in," said Sophia. "We'll decide where we are going on the road."

Odette slipped into the driver's seat. Madison rode shotgun, pistol in hand and resting on her lap. Lifen sat in the back, with Sophia, amongst boxes that belonged to the former owner.

"I don't like the look of those folks," mentioned Madison, gesturing outside.

Sophia crawled forward and peered out the side window to check who she was talking about. Three figures had walked into the park. Two of them, dark-haired men in coats, she did not recognize, but a thinner figure in a kidskin coat made a chill run down her spine. It was the scar-faced man with a patch over his eye—the one who had tried to kill Thomas von Essen in Germany.

"It is that assassin who tried to kill Thomas and me at the tomb," she hissed.

"They're not in their car right now," said Madison. "Why

not just put pedal-to-metal and get out of here? By the time they get to a car, we'll be far away."

Lifen cautioned, "Shhh! They could put a fair bit of lead into this car before we get out of sight."

"We're just going to have to take our chances. We can't let them find us sitting like stupid chickens in the car," Madison insisted.

"Let me remind you, it didn't work out so well for us last time," said Lifen. "They are too close. It's not going to be that hard for them to shoot out a tire."

Lifen had scanned the men in frustration. Sophia had grown tired of their whispered arguments. She spoke, "Shut up, you two! I'm in charge. Let's wait and see if they leave. If they don't, follow my orders."

All four women fell silent. They watched as the three men checked the cars slowly moving amongst them. The scar-faced man made a phone call. He stayed on the phone, staring at how two others steadily moved between the line of different wheels, looking through windscreens. It was only a matter of time before they checked the van. Sophia pondered, hiding them all in the back. She was hoping the men would miss them. Suddenly, she decided against it: if a gunfight did break out, they'd be fish in a barrel. Sophia steeled her nerves, ordering, "Odette, drive!"

"I don't have the keys. I have to start it..." whispered the young French woman.

Sophia replied, worried, "Okay. Start as quickly as you can. Turn down into the alley, weave through the streets to the highway, then turn off as soon as you see the forest. Let's hope we can disappear before they get to us."

Odette carefully arranged the stripped wires, twisting one around the other. She touched two bundles together. There was a crackle of sparks. The starter engine sluggishly heaved over a few times, making a sick chugging sound. The car did not start. Three gunmen looked up. Panic crossed Odette's face. She gritted her teeth and tried again. The vehicle did not start.

"*Il y a un problème... Merde!* We're in a dead car! Get out!"

CHAPTER 20

POISONOUS GIFTS

THE THREE MEN turned their attention to the white van. A handful of cars were all that separated them. The one who spoke on the phone dropped it into his pocket, hurrying towards the van. Sophia could see the gun in his hands. He was gradually approaching the sliding door.

"Get out of driver's side, now! We're sitting ducks! Run, we'll try to find a car we can take later!" shouted Sophia.

Odette scrambled out the door in a panic, followed by Madison. All three men had noticed the movement in the car. As Lifen and Sophia slipped out, the sound of gunfire cut through the cold air. Glass shattered; a dozen holes punched their way through the van. The girls cowered, taking cover behind the newsagent booth. Sophia could feel her heart hammering in her chest. They were at the back of the shop, closed for the night. Sophia nodded to Madison at the entry-way, whispering, "Get us through that!"

Madison didn't question the command. She shouldered her way through that door. It was less sturdy than Madison had imagined, exploding into splinters and leaving her to sprawl onto the floor beyond. The other three women rushed to their new shelter, finding themselves in a storeroom filled with old boxes, *Discover* magazines, wet mops, lottery tickets, and sweet drinks. Madison scrambled up and drew her gun, covering the door. Lighting the flashlight on her phone, Sophia moved into the front of the shop.

"What do you think of this place for making a stand?" she winked to Madison.

"Not good! They can come from multiple angles. The whole front of the shop is made of glass!"

"Damn it! Let's move out, fast! We need to find a car, anyone's car!"

At that moment, Sophia noticed a shabby book under the chair, on the floor. It was the Bible—the book of wisdom and love. Sophia leaned towards, picked it up, and opened it to a random page, praying for advice. She read: *God puts the upright and the sinner to the test, but he has hate in his soul for the lover of violent acts.*

This is not helpful at all, she said to herself, dropping the Bible back on the floor. In the last few days, she felt how her Christian faith had shattered into pieces; it was difficult to behave like a saint when sinners surround you. It was hard to believe in God's words, when you had to run for your life, hiding behind every corner.

———

Dario sat in his car near the highway. He gazed at the scratchy black and white video on his phone. He could see his ex-wife and her companions piling out of a van in panic, cascading through the rear entrance of a newsagent booth. His drone hovered above the scene, moving wherever he told it. It was hard to make out, but Dario was sure he saw the driver's side window shatter. There could be no doubt that the three men in the park were not only pointing guns at them but firing, too. He was annoyed: who were these guys? He was sure they weren't the police. They were trying to kill his wife. He couldn't allow that. If anyone were going to kill her, it would be him... and he was far from finished with her.

Dario made a decision and started his car. He began navigating the streets to get closer to the park, while glancing down to his phone, watching the women leave the shop.

———

A locked metal rolling door barred the front of the newsagent shop. There was nothing for it; they had to break a window. Madison picked up the cash register. She hurled it against the left-hand window, which shattered, spraying glass onto the pavement outside. The girls jumped out, guns in hand.

Madison broke left, bracing herself against the corner of the building. She peered down the alley that led back to the cars. A lonely figure jogged down the lane towards her. She levelled her gun. The man skittered to a halt and lifted his gun. Madison fired first—three loud retorts that echoed through the night streets.

Lifen, Odette, and Sophia ran across the street, taking cover in the opposite alley; its entrance partly blocked by a car. Madison turned from the corner of the building, planning to run after them. A moment later, a dark giant figure stepped around the other side of the shop and drew aim on her. Odette, Lifen, and Sophia levelled pistols on him and fired. As a riot of gunfire broke out, Madison redoubled her speed. She dove over the bonnet of the nearest car, rolling onto the pavement on the other side. The tall man fired at her bravery, blasting out round after round, until a bullet chipped the brick off the wall next to his head. He ducked out of sight.

Madison grinned, her body filled with adrenaline. She sprang up and rushed into the alley, hiding behind the trees, shouting, "Hey, don't just stand there!"

The others followed her.

Odette spoke breathlessly as she ran, "Did you get him? Only two left, right?"

"I got him. I don't know if he's dead, but he won't be doing anything crazy for a while, not with that much shit in his guts!" Lifen answered.

They burst out the other side of the park, checking their backs, fearing they'd see the assassins. They crossed an abandoned street of closed businesses and locked homes. Near an old-fashion fish restaurant stood a car: engine running, interior light on, one door left open. It was a small blue van, the sort you might make food deliveries in. Its driver was nowhere to be seen. After a moment's surprise, the four women ran to the car and climbed in. Odette slipped into the driver's seat. One minute later, they were speeding down the street. They saw how the gunman broke out onto the sidewalk behind them. They happily rounded around the corner and vanished from his sight.

"I can't believe it! A bit of luck for once!" Odette looked up at the heavens. "Don't think that this makes everything even, God-sweetie! You still owe us more!"

"Don't be an idiot, Oddie," said Lifen. "Focus on driving."

Odette navigated the tangle of backstreets, heading onto the highway. Soon, they were streaming through the night-time traffic, driving south, with shadowed farms sweeping by.

Sophia closed her eyes, took deep breaths, and dared to relax a little.

———

From the shadows of a nearby street, Dario watched as the girls found his car, driving away to safety. He was satisfied. He carefully filmed them because he wanted to see Sabina's companions more distinctly. After they were gone, he turned, hurrying back to his car.

———

Mahound stood over one of his men, who lay shivering from shock: three bullet holes in his belly, oozing dark blood. They couldn't take him to a hospital. He had to die here, in the park, in Italy.

Mahound was a very experienced head-hunter. He had never imagined Sophia would prove to be such a challenging quarry. He was one man down. At least now he knew she had companions that were capable of killing. Mahound still couldn't locate Thomas, who seemed to be missing after Istanbul—another loose end.

His phone rang. He picked up, listening to the voice on the other side.

"They found a car, Mahound. A blue panel van with dual back wheels, heading south."

He hung up and called to his team on the highway. They were three of his best men—hopefully, good enough to take care of the situation.

"They're in a blue panel van. Keep an eye out for them on the highway; they might try to take it."

"I'm on it, Mahound. If they come anywhere near us, we'll take care of it," Xander started creeping his car along the edge of the highway, watching the other lines. When he saw how a blue van shot out onto the road, he smiled like a starving predator. Joining the stream of traffic, Xander began following them, saying to his companion, Abbas, who was sitting next to him, "Call Mahound. Tell him we're shadowing them. We'll keep him posted if anything changes."

———

"Where are we going next?" a tired Odette asked.

"Somewhere where we can exchange this car," replied Madison, who was troubled. "Whoever just lost it, is going to call it in pretty fast."

"We'll switch it the next time we see an opportunity," said Sophia, trying to cheer everyone up.

"What we really need is a good place to hide," Lifen added with sarcasm.

———

Xander was careful not to get too close to the van he was following. Sometimes he would slide back a bit further, letting the girls get ahead. He was so discreet that neither he, his companion Abbas, nor the gunman in the back seat, noticed a black sedan with tinted windows following them. They saw it only when a black car cruised up parallel to them, on their right-hand side. They looked at how the windows slid down, and the barrels of two rifles showed up in the air: one from the passenger side, another from the back. Xander's eyes widened in horror. He went to jam his foot on the break, but it was too late. The guns blazed with automatic fire. Xander, Abbas, and their third companion were punched full of holes, spraying the inside of the car with their blood. Their vehicle continued driving across the highway, clipping another car with an explosion of glass. A few seconds later, Xander and his team smashed into the barrier, grinding along for fifty meters before coming to a halt. The black sedan didn't stop. It smoothly accelerated and slowly crept up on the blue van.

———

"Are we being followed?" Lifen asked, worried.

"I don't think so," Odette replied. "It's hard to say, though. We're all moving on the highway, heading in the same direction at the same speed. I suppose some of these cars could be following us. In which case, they were already waiting on the highway...I haven't seen anyone working the traffic to catch up to us."

"Keep a close eye on it, Oddie. We can't afford to be followed," Sophia said.

"We'll know as soon as we turn off. Let's make a few turns. It should become pretty obvious if anyone is following us. Maybe we can set an ambush?" Madison added, stroking her guns. All four girls stiffened as they heard gunfire cut through the sound of traffic.

"*Le coup!* It's happening again!" Odette yelled. "A car behind us just got gunned down by a black sedan. I think they were using real rifles!"

"What the hell is going on?" Madison shouted. "How many cars do we have following us?"

"It might not be anything to do with us," Lifen noticed coldly. "But let's just assume it is and get the hell off this road!"

"If they're after us, then we're just going to suffer the same fate. Soon, very soon." Sophia started to shake. She was hungry and irritated.

"Let's find a way to give them the slip," Odette answered, turning onto a two-lane sealed road that lanced off amidst farmland. A road sign indicated that there was a national park four kilometers ahead. Madison and Odette watched the rear-view mirrors. Sure enough, the black sedan turned off onto the same road as them. It began rapidly gaining ground.

"Do you think you can ever shake them?" Lifen asked, puzzled about their new followers.

"I don't know. *Je suis perdue!* All I've got to work with is this network of country roads. They're faster than us. Maybe if we can make it to the forest..."

It was apparent that any plans of escape were futile. The sedan had inevitably caught up with them: despite Odette's driving skills, it was sitting on their tail. No guns had protruded from it.

"I say I shoot the tires out, and we make our getaway," Madison, proposed looking to Sophia.

"Wait, the car is flashing its headlights. The driver is waving a white handkerchief out of his window," said Odette.

"What the hell do they think they're doing?" Lifen asked. "It's not the oldest trick in the book, but no assassin would expect that to work."

Sophia prepared to leave the car, saying, "Pullover. We're not going to get away. If we start a shooting match, we're outgunned. Everybody, get ready to fight if things go sour."

"This is fuckin' dangerous," Odette mumbled, her voice quavering. "If they come out with guns blazing...Please, don't go!"

"We don't have much choice," said Sophia, stepping out on

the road. "I'm pretty certain that whoever this is, they killed the assassins on our heels. Let's see what they've got to say to us."

Odette nodded, biting her lip. The black sedan pulled over about ten meters away. A man stepped out of the passenger side door, walking forward, holding up his hands. Sophia waited, not moving. Madison was behind her, holding a gun in each hand. She was ready to snap up at a moment's notice. Lifen came down from the other side of the car, with her gun ready. Odette stayed at the wheel.

Sophia walked as far as the back of the van, waiting for the man to come to her, appraising him. He was pretty, blonde, European, and well-groomed in a nice suit. His nose looked like it had been broken many times.

"Hello, Ms. Ferrara. We work for Papa Zen. It's been quite difficult to find you, but luckily for you, we found other men that were hunting you. We've been following them for days. Let me reassure you, we're only here to conduct business. I mean the original business that all of you were hired for."

"I hear you. Thanks. Why don't you tell me what that original business was? While you're at it, get your companions to step out of the car and leave the assault rifles behind. I don't like armed men on the other side of tinted windows," Sophia ordered.

"Fair enough. As long as I have your assurance that everything will stay business and there'll be no gunshots fired from your side."

"You have my word. We're happy to do business. We just need to protect ourselves." Sophia nodded to Madison to check the men when they climbed outside.

The blonde man walked back to the car, followed by Madison. He spoke through the window with people inside. Three men climbed out of the car, allowing Madison to check their clothes and pockets.

The man in charge walked forward, saying, "I'll answer your question, Ms. Ferrara. A man named Thomas was hired by Papa Zen. His goal was to find and retrieve a box hidden in a famous public place in Istanbul. We believe he succeeded but did not survive the attempt. We are here to renegotiate terms."

"You seem to have a grasp of what's happened. I'm listening. What are your terms?" Sophia felt the rush in her blood. They had a real chance to sell the artifact to the original buyer.

"I don't know what you were offered, but Papa was willing to pay at least one million dollars for the box in your possession." Explained the blonde man.

"Thomas is dead. The box is worth a lot more than one million. You won't find it if you search this van. There's only one person who knows where it is."

"We're not here looking for trouble, Ms. Ferrara. If you say that the price has gone up, I don't have the power to negotiate. I can, however, let you talk to Papa himself."

Sophia hesitated, then after a short pause, replied, "Call your boss. I'll talk to him on your phone."

The man punched a number into his phone, held it to his ear, and spoke in a low voice. He extended the phone to Sophia, "It's Papa Zen."

CHAPTER 21

LITTLE RED RIDING HOOD AND PAPA ZEN

SOPHIA: Hello.

Papa Zen: (the voice was gravelly shaped by an Israeli accent) Hello, Sabina! I understand that you have become entangled in the course of horrible, deadly events. I must confess, I am responsible for setting it all in motion. Forgive me.

Sophia: I do not go by the name Sabina anymore. I am dissolving that identity. You can call me Sophia von X. I am the new leader of the 4ASS organization. We are a team of professionals and expect to be treated as such.

Papa Zen: Ha, ha. Okay, Sophia.

Sophia: I understand you have received some photographs of me.

Papa Zen: Ah, I see. You are a woman that likes to get to business. Yes, it is true. I have received some photographs, specifically of a birthmark you possess.

Sophia: Did you offer Thomas fifty-thousand dollars to deliver me to you?

Papa Zen: True. I can assure you...I mean you no harm.

Sophia: Listen up, Papa. Thomas is dead. His people are working for me. I am the only person who knows where the artifact is. Your price is not enough.

Papa Zen: Why is that? I can give you five million. It is good money for a simple Sicilian teacher.

Sophia: Because I have opened the container. I have seen what's inside!

SABINA THOUGHT SHE HEARD PAPA ZEN GROWL IN ANNOYANCE.

Papa Zen: (worried) I hope you have not damaged any of the contents, little girl...

Sophia: I was working at the university. I have been trained to handle old documents. I can assure you I have not damaged anything in the box. It is still in excellent condition. Now that you are aware that I know what I have, can we both agree it's worth more than you're offering, Papa?

Papa Zen: What is your price, Ms. von X?

SOPHIA HESITATED. SHE HAD NOT DISCUSSED WITH HER COMPANIONS WHAT PRICE WOULD BE FEASIBLE. THE LOST PAGES OF THE BIBLE WERE, IN A SENSE, PRICELESS.

Sophia: (with her eyes closed) Fifty million dollars.

Papa Zen: That is a steep price. What makes you think I have that kind of money?

Sophia: Your ability to hire and coordinate teams of mercenaries around the globe.

Papa Zen: (laughed) Tell me what is in the box. If you are right, I'll agree to your price.

SOPHIA LOOKED AT THE MAN IN FRONT OF HER, WONDERING IF SHE WANTED THE WITNESS TO HEAR WHAT SHE WAS ABOUT TO SAY...SHE COULDN'T AFFORD TO SEEM WEAK OR UNCER-

TAIN. SHE NEEDED TO ACT WITH TOTAL CONFIDENCE.

Sophia: The missing pages of the Bible—a code to crack the Book of Revelation.

Papa Zen: Have you told anyone else what you have found?

Sophia: (bluffed) Only my team knows about it. However, I should inform you that the box is not in my possession. The one who holds it, although they do not know what it is, has been instructed to destroy it, in the case of my death or disappearance.

Papa Zen: That is unnecessary, if wise. I am willing to pay your price, my dear von X. I do have a couple of conditions.

Sophia: I'm listening.

Papa Zen: You should come to visit me in Jerusalem. You will be my honored guest. I very much wish to see your birthmark for myself. I'd like to show you personally why it is so significant to me. I will be happy to pay, but in my homeland. Do you accept my invitation?

Sophia: Are you presenting any other option?

Papa Zen: I do not mean to be unreasonable. There is simply no other way I can pay you.

Sophia: Okay. We can meet you in the city of Jerusalem, but I do have my own conditions also.

Papa Zen: Speak.

Sophia: I want a half-million-dollar in advance. If I read your men correctly, they were willing to pay me on the spot, right here, in return for the container. Therefore, they have the money...

Papa Zen: Done.

Sophia: I wish to know who you are. I'm not sure if I can have business dealings with a man whose identity is unknown to me.

Papa Zen: I'm thinking...I can arrange your escort and flight to Jerusalem. My men can keep you safe from any further attempts on your life.

Sophia: I do not mind you going after the assassins who are hunting me, but I must insist that I make my own way to Jerusalem.

Papa Zen: You drive a hard bargain. I do not feel in a position to argue. My men will pay your price. I expect to see you in Jerusalem within the next ten days. My men will leave contact information with you. As to my identity...I will tell you if you agree not to share the information.

Sophia: I will discuss it with nobody apart from my inner circle.

Papa Zen: I am a simple businessman, dear. My name is Jedidiah Ashkenazi.

Sophia: Great. We have an agreement, Mr. Ashkenazi.

Papa Zen: Please, call me Papa. Always.

PAPA ZEN HUNG UP. SOPHIA HANDED THE PHONE BACK TO THE BLONDE MAN. HE NODDED TO HER IN RESPECT, ADDING, "FORGIVE ME, BUT WE WILL HAVE TO WAIT TO RECEIVE ORDERS FROM PAPA. I'M SURE IT WON'T TAKE LONG."

CHAPTER 22

MONEY FLOW

SOPHIA WAS FULL OF TENSION. She glanced back at Madison, who looked deadly serious. She was well aware that despite the promises Papa had made, the order he sent could be anything: to pay, to follow, or to kill them. After the longest two minutes of Sophia's life, a metallic chime broke the stony silence. A swarthy man of Middle Eastern origin, standing by the rear door of the sedan, pulled out his phone. He gazed at the screen, then said in accented English, "We have to pay them the money as negotiated. We also have to leave them. They are free to go. Papa's order."

The blonde man smiled. Sophia saw the relief on his face. He did not wish to receive the order to attack them. After all, he had two guns pointed at him. He spoke, "Seems you can continue your journey, Ms. Ferrara. Would you like the money in cash or credit?"

"I'll take two-hundred-thousand dollars in cash and have the rest in credit."

Lifen came forward. She held out her phone with bank account details on the screen. The blonde man copied it down.

The swarthy man with a strange accent opened a briefcase on the back seat of the sedan. He took out twenty bound wads of bills, walked over, and placed them in Sophia's hands.

"The money will be in your account soon," announced the blonde man.

"I believe that concludes our business, gentlemen," Sophia replied, trying to sound as cool as possible.

Both groups climbed into their cars. Odette pulled away, waving her middle finger to the black sedan. For a while, the four women sat in silence, cruising down the country lane.

"Fuck! That went better than I thought it would," Madison suddenly giggled. "What's our next move?"

Sophia said, "We need to arrange a flight to Jerusalem. Ideally, it would be great if we could take our firearms and equipment." She paused, looking at Odette, "Your job will be to find out as much as you can about Jedidiah Ashkenazi. I hope he hasn't provided us with a false name, but you never know."

"It's going to be hard to tell," speculated a happy Odette. "He could provide us with another man's identity. I'd say until we're standing right in front of him, how would we know?"

"I see what you mean," Sophia replied, rechecking the bank account.

"There's nothing we can do about it...just like there's little we can do to stop him from preparing to ambush or betray us. On the other side, he did pay us in advance. He can't know what contingencies we've got in place. We could easily arrange third parties to take revenge or expose the truth if anything happens to us."

"All we can do is trust that he's sane and reasonable. I think Papa wants this to stay quiet," said Lifen, while counting the money in the back.

Sophia and her companions were exhausted when they arrived in Caserta one and a half-hour later. It was dark; the city was sleeping. They found a quiet three-star hotel with a charming name, StellaMari. It was located on Via di Vigna, surrounded by stunning rocky hills and the famous cross del Giubileo di Casola. After the sleepy clerk handed them their keys, the four girls parked the van out of sight and went up to their room for much-needed rest. The room was spacious, with two beds. They decided that one should stay guard. Madison took the first round. She couldn't sleep anyway. She sat in the dark hotel room, staring at her glowing laptop. Madison tried to find a private jet that could discreetly fly the four of them with unchecked baggage out of the country. She could ask Lifen for help, but she didn't want to bother her. Today, in the middle of the driving chaos, she found out that Lifen is pregnant. Only by chance, she saw the chat on Lifen's phone: an odd conversation between her and Asha. In his messages, Asha demanded to know who is that animal, and when Lifen is planning to tell her family about it. The last SMS from Lifen included only one name—*Thomas von Essen.*

CHAPTER 23

A DESPICABLE FATE

IT WAS dangerous to steal a car, but given the circumstances, Dario, normally a meticulous planner, had little choice. He thought allowing Sabina and her companions to stumble upon his van was brilliant. It allowed them to escape the killers that he doubted he could overpower. It also allowed him to keep tracking all of Sabina's movements. Unfortunately, Dario's old car couldn't keep up with the race. He made a spontaneous decision.

He was unable to pick locks or hotwire cars. That's why he loitered in the car park behind the bar, where the girls had been staying. He held an inebriated revel maker at gunpoint when two women stumbled back to their car. He prepared to wait. He learned how to wait many years ago when he chased young and innocent Sabina Ferrara. Finally, the girls left. Dario took the keys, intimidated the man into climbing in his boot, then drove out of town. Once isolated, he secured the man's hands and feet with zip ties. He gagged his mouth one more time, enjoying the picture. Satisfied with his handy work, Dario climbed back into the driver's seat. He checked Sabina's location on his phone, then started the car. It was time to have a long-awaited conversation.

Dario passed a grey sedan riddled with bullet holes. Two highway patrol cars were pulled over next to it. Police officers were standing around the car grave faced. He thought it was too much of a coincidence to be unrelated to the gun runners hunting his wife. The tracker indicated that his van had pulled off the highway and stopped on an isolated country road. Dario couldn't believe they would sleep in his van so close to the gunmen they had just fled.

No, they must be talking strategy, he thought to himself. He noticed that they quickly moved on. He followed them to the city called Caserta. The tracker showed they had driven to a small three-star hotel—StellaMari. His blue van had sat there for the last thirty minutes. Dario smiled; they had stopped for the night. He pulled up outside the StellaMari hotel, parking on the street. He stepped out into the cold night air, shrugging his jacket on, and folding up the collar. He trudged over to the double glass doors at the front of the hotel, only to find them secured. He could see an unattended reception. Annoyed, he called the hotel. After a few rings, someone picked up. An angry male voice said, "Hello, this is StellaMari hotel. How may I help you?"

"My name is Bob Calvary. I'm at the front door of your hotel, which says it has vacancies, but everything is locked up," explained Dario.

"Yes, yes, one minute. I will be there shortly, Sir."

Two minutes later, a young man with a mop of dark hair unlocked the door, letting Dario into the foyer.

"We're a very small hotel, Sir. We don't often get visitors at night. Most people book ahead. You're lucky we have a couple of rooms free," the hotel clerk said.

Dario smirked, holding ten bucks between his fingers, "I was wondering if my wife were here. She would have arrived in a blue van about forty minutes ago."

The young man spoke cautiously as he walked around the desk, "Yeah, some women arrived in a blue van today. They didn't mention they were expecting company or a husband."

Dario shrugged innocently, "They must be tired. I told her I'd arrive tonight. Her name is Sophia. Which room is she in?"

"I can't tell you that, Sir," the clerk carefully took the money. "But I can give her a call. I can tell your wife that you're here."

"At this time of night? My wife would be furious! You don't know that witch! Why not just give me a key? I'll let myself in..."

The young man shook his head, increasingly suspicious. Dario's patience was running out. He could see that the computer was unlocked. Everything he needed to know was only a few keystrokes away. It would be easy enough to overpower the young clerk. The only thing that made him hesitate was the camera watching the foyer: it would witness his crime. He had to decide if the CCTV had an internal link or if it fed to an external security company. Dario thought, *This place is pretty cheap. I doubt they'd invite additional expenses. I bet that camera is fake, or at best, linked to a nearby computer.*

He smiled again, "You're right, why not give them a call. If she's angry, I'll just blame it on you," he gave a humorless laugh.

The clerk laughed with him, then picked up the phone. Without any warning, Dario grabbed the boy by the hair. He violently drove his head down into the desk with a sickening thud. The clerk fumbled to push the desk away, but Dario was much stronger. He lifted the clerk's head and drove it down again, and again, and again...pulping his young face, smearing blood across the desk. The man shuddered and went limp. Dario let his tangle of dark hair slide through his fingers.

Sweating, but fully satisfied, Dario walked around the desk. He heaved the clerk's body off the counter, onto the floor. He sat down, searching the hotel's records. There it is: room twenty-two. *Just one room for all four women? They must be packed in there like sardine., I'll have to be careful*, Dario thought to himself.

He walked back to his car, wiped for prints, took his bag, re-entered the hotel and locked the doors behind him. He walked over to the office behind the desk. To his satisfaction, he found a second computer displaying camera feeds. On the wall, he noticed a series of numbered hooks holding spare keys for the rooms. He took the key to room twenty-two. He wiped the computer and downloaded the software that would be perfect for his task. He also removed and pocketed the disk that had been recording his activities. Everything took only ten minutes. He walked back out into the foyer and checked the young man's pulse. He was still alive. His face was puffy and split, bubbles of blood-formed as he breathed. Dario stood over the body, pondering whether to kill him or just tie him up. *I bet he doesn't have the money to fix that face. He'll have to get used to looking like a freak...I'll bet he never trusts another human again. He can live. I prefer him that way.*

———

Lifen woke up. It was her turn to guard the door. She made coffee and checked her phone. Zero messages. She sunk in an armchair, tapping away at her laptop. Several businesses, private owners, nieces, and uncles had answered her emails, but nothing from Asha.

Sophia and Odette were already asleep. They shared the double bed, exhausted by their ordeal. Madison slept on the small bed, close to the floor, tossing and turning.

Without warning, the door swung open. A bulky figure silhouetted in the frame. Lifen began pushing herself up out of the chair—then froze. She saw the light gleaming off the chromed revolver. The unknown man was pointing a gun at her. He said, "Don't move."

She looked desperately over at the bed, but neither of the women had woken.

Madison's eyes sprang open. She sat upright, but only to find the gun pointed at her and Lifen. The man hissed, "Don't move a muscle. If either of you does anything other than what I say, I won't hesitate to shoot you. Do you understand, bitches?"

Madison sat glaring at the man. He wore jeans, a leather jacket, and had a thick unkempt brown beard. There was an air of confidence and smugness about him. That made Madison loathe him; that left no doubt in her mind, he would happily shoot her if she stepped out of line.

"I'm here for one of you. Sabina."

"Why do you want her? If it's money you want, we can pay you," said Lifen.

Dario sneered, "I'm not interested in your money. You will either cooperate or die - the choice is yours."

Sophia stirred, awakened by the sound of voices. It was dark. She propped herself up and peered around the room. She could see Lifen's fearful face in the glow of her laptop. Madison was sitting on her bed. There was another figure by the door.

Sophia couldn't make it out, but something about that silhouette was chilling.

"What's going on?" she asked.

The room flooded with light. The man flicked the switch by the door. Sophia stared in disbelief at Dario, who was standing and grinning, in the same hotel room. He levelled his revolver on her. She let out a cry of despair. Odette woke up last. She rolled over, facing the gun.

Dario spoke, "This is how it's going to work, wife. You're going to get up, and you're going to come with me. If any of you try to stop me, I'm going to shoot you dead. Is that crystal clear?"

Sophia was in shock. She could not comprehend how Dario was standing here, in Caserta. She glanced over at the other girls. None of them were in hands reach of a gun.

"Okay. I'll come with you," said Sophia, climbing out of bed. She wore a white t-shirt and pink underwear. She hated the smile that spread on Dario's lips when he saw her half-dressed.

She forced herself to keep speaking, "These women have been holding me hostage. They keep saying they'll let me go when this is over, but it never seems to be over..."

"I see. I guess I'm your Knight in Shining Armour, Darling. Come with me."

The Sicilian woman walked over to her husband. He grinned at her for a moment, then said, "Turn around and face the room."

Sophia wanted to attack him, she was close enough, but something about his presence paralyzed her. She was still reeling from him being here, still trying to make sense of the situation. She didn't trust herself. She didn't know if she'd be able to fight and kill him, so she turned around as she was told.

Dario pulled her arms behind and zip tied her wrists. He shoved her on the floor. She fell heavily, groaning from the impact. Madison rolled to her feet but froze again when the gun pointed on her. Dario was fast.

"You're a feisty one. You can be next...Lie on your face."

For a moment, Sophia thought Madison was going to punch him, but instead, she lay down, clenching her jaw. Dario zip tied her hands and feet. He did the same to Lifen, pushing her on the floor, next to Madison. He tied Odette on the bed, fully naked. Satisfied with the view, he dragged his wife out of the room.

Sophia knew she couldn't call for help. She couldn't afford the attention of the police. Even worse, she had no idea why Dario was here. It felt like a nightmare. She stared at the leering face of her ex-husband as he guided her downstairs. He dragged her in her underwear into the chill of the rear car parking. They walked over to the blue van they'd arrived in.

"I don't have the keys," she stammered.

"Don't worry. I do. It's my car, after all."

Unlocking the car, Dario slid open the side door and bundled his ex-wife inside. He climbed into the driver's seat and slowly pulled out of the hotel parking, driving north.

———

Lying in the darkness, Sophia came to the full realization that Dario had let her find this vehicle; he had fitted it with a tracking device. Not only that, but he probably had also traced her call. She understood that he was not just a narcissistic oaf, he was far more skilled and far more dangerous than she had ever suspected. Somehow, it made it all worse. He not only had mistreated her, but he'd also concealed from her whole sections of his life. She had never really known him. Dario had manipulated her from the very first day they met.

"Why are you doing this?" Sophia asked from the back.

"You are my wife. I was waiting for you to come crawling back, but it seems you got caught up in all this bullshit. I'm here to bring you home. By the way, I love your new hair color. Plum, very sexy."

"I can't go home. They'll lock me up, Dario."

"I suppose that's true," he chuckled. "I've got the money you don't know about. It's enough to find a tiny place, out of the way, where people can't identify you. You'll be safe...as long as you're a good girl."

Dario fell silent, revelling as the full weight of his plans slowly soaked into Sophia's brain. He knew she'd thought she'd escaped, but that choice was never hers to make.

Sophia lay, uncomfortable and cold on the bare metal floor, her mind churning. The horror of Dario's plan was beginning to sink in. She would be his slave. He would hold over her the fact that, at any moment, he could call the authorities. She would be imprisoned for the rest of her life. He would no doubt call the police to take care of Lifen, Madison, and Odette, who had no idea who he was or where he'd gone. She had to escape but couldn't do that tied up.

———

Back in the hotel room, Madison shouted, "Who the fuck was that? Why did he leave us alive?"

"Who cares? We need to get free of these ties! We have to get out of here," said Lifen, rolling on the floor.

"*AU SECOURS!* It's so cold," said Odette, shaking. "That fella might have been Sophia's ex-husband. She said he was big, with a huge brown beard. Did you see how scared she was? She had the same look she sometimes gets when she talks about him!"

"Shit, he really did trace that call!" Lifen added. The idea of lying on the dirty motel floor in white-laced lingerie made her mind scream.

"We can't hold it against her. We all come with a past and baggage," Madison said. She strained against the zip tie, but all it did was bite painfully into her flesh. She worked her way over to her clothes. First, she pulled them off the chair with her teeth, then rolled on top until she found the flick knife in her pocket. She freed herself and her mates. With no more need to speak, they all quickly dressed, packed, and descended the rear stairwell to the parking lot.

Their van was missing.

"That bastard took our van!" exclaimed Odette in disbelief.

"Fine! Take another one!" Lifen fumed.

Odette picked an old Toyota model. She popped the door open and a minute later started the car. The road was empty.

"We have to rescue Sophia. Yes, I know, I know, we have no idea where they are. She also has nothing we could use to trace her. That horrible man dragged her out in her underwear. What's going on with the world?!?" Odette said from the driver seat.

Madison answered, watching the road with sadness, "He was here to find her. He didn't even ask about the box. Fuckin' demon from Sophia's past! I hate him! Lin, what do you think? Where should we start looking?"

"We can't find her. We don't know where he is going. We have to trust that she'll escape and call us. When she does, we need to be ready. That's all we can do right now. Let's find a place to park, plug our phones in to charge and try to get some rest. There's no point to rush anywhere tonight," Lifen said, closing the conversation.

Odette drove the car to the nearest farm, Cancello Scalo, trying to figure out who is the Boss now. They stopped on the tiny Via Ischitella, hiding between the high walls of the ranch and the deserted fields of durum wheat.

CHAPTER 24

OUTSIDE OF REALITY

DARIO SKILFULLY NAVIGATED the van through the enveloping darkness. The rhythmic hum of the engine and the sporadic rustling of leaves were the only companions in the stillness of the night. He glanced at the woman's motionless silhouette inside his van at times. She appeared lifeless, yet he could hear her breathing and observe her shivers. The idea of draping his jacket over crossed his mind, but he ultimately dismissed it. *Enough of this,* he mused silently. *It's time for her to understand that I embody cruelty itself.*

Dario was exceeding the speed limit. He was angry; he felt the journey was taking him farther from his destination. He craved respite from the long night. As frustration threatened to overcome him, he entered into a familiar tunnel. On the other side, the landscape underwent a remarkable transformation, and a small signpost welcomed him to Melizzano.

"At last," Dario whispered under his breath.

Melizzano, a small countryside, presented a picturesque outlook of rolling hills adorned with vibrant colors. Majestic trees stood tall, their branches creating a natural canopy over-head. The first rays of the morning sun gently filtered through the leaves, casting a mesmerizing play of light and shadows. The air was filled with the sweet fragrance of blooming, and the distant sound of a babbling brook added a soothing melody to the serene atmosphere. Quaint farmhouses dotted the land-scape as he continued driving, each exuding a timeless charm that beckoned him to continue further into the countryside.

The muffled sounds emanating from the woman in his van snagged his attention.

"What's the matter now, Sabina?" He called her by her actual name, unwinding her from the constraints of the Sophia facade she used to hide her identity.

Another attempt escaped her lips - a desperate plea to tell him something. Deliberately, he hesitated to peel off the tape, relishing the opportunity to toy with her further. As she wearied from the effort, he finally relented, slowing down and turning toward her, ripping the duct tape open.

"Ow! That hurts," Sabina winced.

"What do you want? And don't try to scream; there's no one around."

"I need to go to the toilet, please."

Dario surveyed her nearly naked form with a mean smirk, "You could go in here; I don't mind. Or you could tough it out for a few more minutes. We're almost there."

Without awaiting a response, he clumsily fumbled to reapply the tape over her mouth.

Dario stopped the van as they got to a secluded part of Melizzano. He decided to take a break and turned off the igni-tion. The engine's growl faded, giving way to the serene ambiance of the countryside. Birds serenaded from the treetops. The crisp air embraced their song, carrying a subtle fragrance of earth that added a rustic charm to the tranquil scene.

Dario's face morphed into a stern expression.

"Oi, Sabina, I'm going to remove the tape. Be quiet, okay?"

The woman nodded. Dario peeled away the tape that had stifled her voice, unveiling the fatigue across her face. Then he stepped out of the van, circling to the opposite side with a gallant gesture. He opened the door, untied Sabina's legs, and guided her out of the vehicle.

"Handle your business right here," he directed, gesturing to the ground beside the van, his fingers subtly grazing the handle of the holstered gun.

Sophia met his directive with a quizzical gaze. "I can't do it right here..."

"Do you see a fucking restroom nearby?" Dario retorted, a trace of impatience seeping into his words. "Hurry the fuck up."

"Face the other way," Sophia countered.

Dario chuckled. "You're my wife; why bother turning around?"

Sophia hesitated. Dario pivoted to scan their surroundings, not out of courtesy but to ensure no unwanted guests lurked nearby.

"I'm done," Sabina said.

Dario placed a strip of duct tape over her mouth, silencing her once more as he briskly tossed her back into the van. Once inside, he locked the doors, the distinct metallic clink echoing through the confined space, and deftly stowed the van's key in the right pocket of his pants.

"It's time for some rest," Dario declared. "We've got a lot more on our plate."

. . .

In the quiet of the morning, a knock echoed through the van. Dario's eyes widened in surprise when he saw a man of medium build with salt-and-pepper hair neatly combed to the side standing in front of the truck. His olive skin suggested a life spent outdoors. Dressed in the official postman uniform, he wore a crisp blue shirt adorned with the postal service emblem and sturdy black trousers.

Dario hadn't noticed they had parked near the post office, and now, the local postman stood at his door with a curious expression. Dario motioned for Sophia to remain silent and stepped outside.

"Hi there! I'm Angelo Correti," the postman introduced himself.

"Dexter. Any issue, Mr. Correti?"

"I noticed your van is sitting here for a while. Is there a problem?"

"No problems," Dario assured. "I'm just taking a breather after a lengthy drive out of town. We'll be on our way shortly."

"New to town, then?" Angelo pondered.

Suppressing his frustration, Dario kept his composure. "Not exactly. I come and go. I recently inherited a house from my late aunt, Betti. We're headed there; my wife is still asleep."

He nodded towards the van.

"Condolences for your loss," Angelo replied.

Strange moans reached Angelo's ears, a hint of concern furrowing his brows. "Did you hear something, Mister Dexter? Everything is alright?"

"Oh, that? It's my wife, Lucia. She tends to get a bit queasy during long drives. And she's pregnant, too. Morning sickness, you know?" Dario offered a friendly smile.

"Pregnant?"

"Yeah, she's pregnant. Doctors said it's normal. I hoped to find a quiet place for her to relax, away from the road's bumps and all." Dario explained nervously.

"Congratulations on the upcoming addition to your family," the postman remarked, attempting to maintain a friendly tone. "If you need a peaceful spot, Casa Acqua is around the bend—a perfect place for moments like these."

"Thanks, Angelo. We should get going before my wife gets too uncomfortable."

"Of course. If you do decide to go there, ask for Siniora Eleonora. She can help your wife if necessary. Wishing you a smooth journey and all the best with the little one on the way." Angelo waved to the road.

"Much appreciated," Dario expressed, firmly clasping the man's hand. He had picked up the art of a firm handshake as a subtle, effective means of conveying confidence, or in this case, intimidation.

Dario got in, inserted the key, and turned it, but the van emitted a reluctant sputter. Cursing, he tried again, and the engine roared to life under his command. Offering a tight-lipped smile to Angelo, who stood and looked at him, Dario steered the van towards Casa Aqua, which was a supposed mere ten-minute drive away, pretending that was his intended destination.

The wheels churned the gravel. Dario's gaze flickered to the rear-view mirror and saw how Angelo retrieved his phone, capturing images of the van. Dario felt anger smoldering within as he considered his options. Pressing on the accelerator, he decided not to confront the postman, avoiding drawing unnecessary attention to himself during this time of the day.

He maneuvered the car to the Morcone area instead of Casa Aqua.

Dario navigated the road with a sense of urgency; his mind raced with thoughts of his next move. He spotted a small, weathered gas station on a quiet village's outskirts. He brought the van to a halt before the gas station and glanced back at his captive, who maintained an uneasy silence. The woman was glaring at him, but he didn't mind. As long as she didn't try anything stupid, they were good. Dario climbed out of the van and pulled out the fuel nozzle. He checked his environment, ensuring the absence of any unwelcome presence. Content with his surroundings, he shifted his attention back to the car.

He heard familiar muffled cries. An exasperated groan escaped him as he slid into the van, fixing his gaze on the half-naked body.

"What's again?" he inquired. "You're a real pain. Keep it down, or I might have to use this." He gestured with his gun near the woman's face.

"We've been on the roads for hours. I'm starving," Sabina complained.

"I have no time for this bullshit. We'll talk more when I arrive in Campollataro Park," Dario silenced her by reapplying the tape, vowing not to remove it again until they reached their destination.

Resuming the journey, Dario turned onto a narrow road leading to the camping houses near Lago di Campolattaro. The daylight danced through the foliage, casting dappled shadows on the road. The van rolled along. The engine's steady purr supported Dario's contemplation of the challenge ahead.

After fifteen minutes, Dario arrived at Lago di Campolattaro Park. The camping houses were nestled together like close friends and had slanted roofs. Sturdy wood made them appear strong, with windows that wore flower boxes like fancy hats. Every house had its style – some were bright and cheerful, others - quieter and darker. Dario experienced a mix of relief and apprehension. He stopped and climbed out of the van. Birds chirped in the distance, and a gentle breeze rustled the leaves, creating an illusion of tranquillity.

CHAPTER 25

ONE DEAD BULLY

SOPHIA'S MIND had been racing throughout the long drive to Lago di Campolattaro Park, brainstorming escape plans. Eventually, Dario guided her out of the van, leading her into one of the camping houses. It was the smallest one on the base. He pushed his wife inside the tiny restroom and turned to lock the door. Her mouth remained taped shut.

"Here's your chance for a proper bathroom break," Dario chuckled.

The woman scanned the bathroom for a potential weapon against Dario, but all she found was a white towel hanging from a bar and tissue paper on a wall-mounted holder near the toilet. She let out an exasperated groan, frustration evident in the furrow of her brows. Turning towards the solitary window in the bathroom, she anxiously bit her lips, contemplating her escape. The idea of slipping through it seemed plausible. Sophia fumbled with the net on the window, but the task proved more challenging than anticipated. A sudden knock on the bathroom door jolted her.

"Are you giving birth in there?" Dario's voice echoed through the door.

Sophia closed the net with caution and descended. After washing her hands, she stepped out to face her suspicious husband.

Sophia sat on the chair and observed Dario's purposeful stride as he marched towards the compact kitchen. He grabbed a bottle of whiskey to satisfy his thirst.

"You want some?" Dario offered.

Sophia nodded in agreement.

"Here you go, darling," Dario said.

He removed the duct tape, allowing her to drink. After that, with a bottle in his hand, he rummaged through the kitchen cupboard in search of sustenance, only to find it disappointingly bare. His eyes turned toward a small refrigerator. Dario opened it. Inside, he found a carton of cereal and a gallon of milk. He prepared the cereal in a bowl and started eating, devouring it with unbridled hunger.

After the meal, Dario roughly pulled Sophia away from the chair, tossing her onto a small sofa like a ragdoll. He unzipped his jeans.

"Time to pay for all the troubles you've cost me, bitch," he hissed.

Sophia's cry echoed through the air of the camping house. Just as her husband began to force himself upon her, the door exploded open. Two bulky figures entered the house. Both young and quick, they seized control of the room. One man grabbed Dario from behind, restraining his neck and hands, while the other, wielding a knife, thrust it into Dario's stomach. The injured man crumpled to his knees, clutching his bleeding stomach. Shocked, Sophia watched as a small woman entered and began methodically cleaning the pool of blood on the floor.

One of the men injected Sophia's husband with a needle, causing him to lose consciousness. Dario's body collapsed to the floor with an alarming thud. The two men exited the scene, engaging in a short conversation with two others outside. These newcomers entered the house and removed Dario's limp form from the room, placing it in a waiting car.

The man who had stabbed Dario returned.

"Relax, this will only sting a bit," he reassured as he injected Sophia with the needle. A fuzzy sensation enveloped her. He lifted her, tossing her over his shoulder. The ground spun in Sophia's eyes when they marched out of the house. The man placed her into a black Mercedes. Before succumbing to unconsciousness, Sophia caught the sight of Dario's lifeless body on the grass.

Sophia's opened her eyes. She could hear a jumbled voice speaking far away, and as the fog dissipated, she heard him more clearly. It was the man who had drugged her; he spoke on the phone.

"The woman's a witness, boss. What's the plan for her?" he paused, then responded. "Sure thing."

The man turned towards the woman and pressed on the speaker.

"Hello, I'm Don Alfonso. And you are?"

"I'm Sophia... Sorry, Sabina Ferrara."

A chuckle resonated from the other end. "Drop the dual personality act, Sabina. You are Matteo's sister, right?"

"Yes, I'm his sister."

"Accept my condolences," Don Alfonso offered. "Your

brother was family, and we've been relentlessly pursuing his killer, Dario, for a while now."

The message hit her. She had suspected Dario's involvement in her brother's death, but without concrete evidence, the puzzle remained incomplete.

"I suspected that he was the one who did it," Sophia admitted. Her voice was trembling with a surge of emotions.

"Your suspicion was right. Dario killed Matteo and left him on the floor of your house... to rot. Until we found him."

"Dario must pay for his crime!" Sophia said.

Don Alfonso's voice remained calm, "You have my word. We will make an example out of your husband. He won't escape the consequences of what he did to Matteo."

"Make him suffer, please," she begged.

A sinister undertone crept into Alfonso's following words, "We're bringing him back to our hometown. I assure you that he won't find peace. He'd be kept alive for some days, and each day, we'd remove a part of his body, twenty-four pieces for Matteo's twenty-four years. He'll beg to die, don't worry."

"Thank you, Don Alfonso. "You saved me from unimaginable agony," Sophia said, her voice filled with genuine gratitude. "Thank you for bringing Dario to justice, but I need your help. I have to be in Jerusalem in nine days."

"Jerusalem? Why there?" Don questioned, curious.

Sophia hesitated, avoiding the question. "I can't explain, but I need to go there. Please."

"I've already helped you by sparing your life as you witnessed our business. A little honesty wouldn't hurt."

"I need to meet my team. Have you heard about us? 4ASS."

Don Alfonso, a bit annoyed, sighed but eventually

relented. "Yes. I know about them... Fine, I'll help you, but remember this favor." He paused. "Or better make it two."

"Thank you, Don Alfonso," Sophia said. "When can I be on my way?"

"I need you to lay low for a week while we'll arrange your transfer to Jerusalem."

Sophia understood the terms of this uneasy alliance well. She hesitated but then asked, "I am on the wanted list by the Italian and Turkish police and Interpol."

"Aren't we all? Go with my boys... we always need an extra cleaner." Don Alfonso laughed and instructed his man, "Gustavo, make sure she's alright."

"Si, Don Alfonso."

The connection severed abruptly, leaving Sophia with a surprising calmness, replacing her initial fear of Gustavo.

"I apologize for the earlier misunderstanding." Gustavo smiled.

"No problems, Gus," she responded. "Lead the way."

CHAPTER 26

———

THE HOLY CITY

THE DAY WAS GROWING old as the jet circled The Ben Gurion airport. Lifen, Madison, and Odette sat in first class, each with a private booth, trapped with their thoughts. Odette was the least worried, she idly watched the jumbled airport turning beneath her as the plane spiraled down to land. It was tiny compared to the immense place they had escaped in Istanbul. She was thrilled that Sophia had managed to outsmart her captor, but curious how she had managed to make it to the holy city before them. Lifen watched the dense muddle of cars oozing in and out of the endless roads. In her mind, she toyed with different scenarios: could this be a trap; could the phone call they received have been false or under coercion; what to do with the life that had been growing inside of her—the child of dead Thomas von Essen; how to tell Sophia about it? Madison chewed her lip. During the whole flight, she was tense and nervous. She was scared that Sophia would punish her, punish all of them, for not managing to find and rescue her. After all, she was their leader.

Soon the plane touched down. It trucked to a halt close to

the main building. Smiling air hostesses ushered each of the women out of their booths. Three girls disembarked along with everyone else from first class. They crossed the forecourt and entered the main building. There, they were immediately swallowed in a bustling crowd of people, striving to file through to the exit or jostling to get to the slow river of baggage on the conveyor belt.

The 4ASS team made their way to the luggage, looking for their bags. Odette studied the everchanging crowd, searching for a familiar face but seeing none. Soon they moved through airport security, where a gloomy faced man in a khaki uniform watched each girl like a hawk as they walked through a scanner. None had been foolish enough to wear suspicious items.

All three moved out into the exit. The architecture of the arrival hall was spectacularly beautiful and inspiring: elegantly designed walls, a rare selection of bronze statues, flowering gardens dipped in grapes, dates, and olives. People stood around holding signs, a few of them written in English. United families embraced each other, laughing; loved ones wept to see dear faces.

———

Sophia watched her team across the bustling hall. It did not surprise her that they hadn't recognized her. She was not wearing one of her customary country-style dresses. She had chosen a pragmatic outfit: black jeans, a blue blouse, Nike cross-trainers, white cap, and Dior sunglasses. She also dyed her hair light brown.

The girls looked good. Lifen, as always, was dressed like she was about to attend a lavish secret party for super rich celebs. Her white silk dress from Armani matched her Louboutin heels. Her hands were fully dotted with gold jewelry. She wore a broad black hat to help with the heat. The funniest thing were her eyes—the lenses she wore were pitch black. *Well, she could have been a zombie star. Or the luxury meal*, Sophia thought.

Madison was dressed as practically as usual, in jeans and a white t-shirt. Her stride, confident; her eyes, alert. Odette wore a long flowing green dress, buttoned up in the front, but undone below the hips, to flash her legs, while she walked. On her nose sat round sunglasses. Sophia thought she looked strained. *I wonder what's getting under her skin? Or maybe she's as nervous about moving this hot potato as I am?* Sophia asked herself. She pushed off the wall, slowly walking through the crowd.

Odette was the first to spot her. She nudged Madison in the back, whispering where to look. Madison turned to meet their leader. Sophia noticed relief mixed with fear on the face of her American mate.

"There she is," said Odette.

They all stopped, focusing on her.

"There you are," said Lifen, inspecting Sophia up and down appraisingly. "I must admit I was prepared for the worst, but you are in good shape, von X."

Sophia's answer was crisp and cold. "Yes, I'm fine. We'll talk more once we are outside."

Sophia led them through the doors, into the pickup area. She had lied. She was not okay! She was tired of so many days of fear and constant focus. Her body ached from the bruises her fight with Dario had left behind. But...she was alive. She was determined never to let another man make her his slave.

. . .

The four women moved past the ranks of slowly maneuvering taxis. As they walked in the shade, cast down by the bowing trees, Sophia spoke, "I guess it was one of you that called the police."

"It was me!" stammered Madison. "I hoped it would help. I couldn't think of anything else I could do. I called as anonymous and said you'd been snatched. Sorry, I gave them your false name—Maria Sophia von Poison."

Madison told her how she monitored the police channels, how she thought they might catch up with her. She told her about everything they've done to be able to get closer to Dario, but it didn't work out.

Sophia rolled her eyes. "Don't be so hard on yourself, Mad. You did the best you could. As it is, police harassment caused him to abandon the car, which ultimately allowed me to run away."

"Did you kill the psycho?" asked Odette.

Sophia shook her head. "I would love to, but the opportunity didn't present itself. The police took him. Revenge is a dish best served cold; he'll get his comeuppance." She paused and hid her face inside of her palms. "He killed my brother. I have to make him suffer!"

There was a long silence: Sophia's jaw going up and down, as she wanted to speak. A few seconds later, the Sicilian woman dropped her hands down and, without another word, continued her walk.

"Well, you can tell us more later. What matters right now is moving the pages and mobilizing with the money we gain," said Lifen, more quickly than usual. "What have you arranged already?"

Lifen felt bloated and heavy. She was still using the same

size clothes but developed some kind of phobia of becoming fat.

Sophia put on a fake bright voice: "I've talked with Papa Zen on the phone. He arranged a meeting with one of his men in half an hour. That man, Abush, will take us to a secure place, near Ben Shemen Forest. Papa has agreed to exchange payment for the Hagia box today. Only today! I understand we don't have much leverage or backup, but I believe we should try."

"Worse than that," replied Madison, running her fingers through her blonde hair, "we don't have guns. If something goes wrong, we're going to have to kick our way out of there like in some bad Kung Fu movie."

"I don't like the sound of this," Odette said. "The best advice I'll give you—let's go to Tel Aviv, lay low, and come back when we're ready."

"We won't be walking into this meeting unarmed," Sophia smiled mysteriously. "Papa Zen will lose his good graces if we try to drag this out. I'm hoping he wants to keep things quiet. If one of the three of you has a better idea, now is the time to say it."

Lifen agreed with Sophia. She wanted to tell her about Thomas and her baby, but too many things were at stake. She couldn't risk losing the trust of her group by playing a sick, pregnant cow.

"Where are these guns?" asked Madison, curious.

"In my car." Sophia pointed out a white family car—its paint chipped and bodywork dented. Sophia opened the boot, unzipped a duffel bag. Madison smiled when she saw pistols, clips, boxes of ammunition, and two pump-action shotguns accompanied by leather belts of shells.

"Great Arsenal, babe!" she slammed Sophia's back with

respect. "How on earth did you get all this? How did you slip out of Italy? I can't figure it out—how could a fragile woman like you come to Jerusalem and then get your hands on all these yummy guns?"

"It's a long story...," said Sophia with a mystical smile. "Maybe I'll tell you one day, when we're high. I mean—never. Enough chatting. Follow me."

Sophia led the way to the WC block for tourists. The members of 4ASS approached the low brick building. They stepped inside and closed the metal door. They unpack the guns Sophia had mysteriously acquired. There were four derringers and some tiny pistols, made for concealment, which fired a single heavy round. Odette and Lifen put chosen guns in their handbags. Madison slipped hers into the pocket and backpack. Sophia took the time to strap on an ankle holster. She looked at the bag with the guns one more time. Too many were left. She pushed a spare Glock into the back of her belt.

"Better leave the rest in the car," said Madison. "I doubt Papa is so stupid that he is going to let us in, hiding two-three guns under our clothes!"

Sophia smiled, "Two is a lucky number. I need two, just in case."

It was time to make contact with the enigmatic Jedidiah Ashkenazi. Two messages arrived on Sophia's phone. The first message was from Abush:

Meet me at a small gas station Al-Bin-Raki, near Ben Shemen Forest.

The second message came from the unknown number:

If everything goes as planned, you'll meet Papa within an hour.

Sophia read the info aloud, explaining, "It is the best we

could hope for as it's a forty-minute drive into the heart of Jerusalem. I'm driving."

———

The members of 4ASS sped past small townships, sports shops, parks, and bridges. They navigated towards the holy city. After fifteen minutes, they turned off at a small petrol station: it was busy with no spare parking. The tables of vendors, selling fruit and canned drinks to the side of the forecourt were crowded with tourists. Sophia reminded herself that it was the time for the Passover Festival—the busiest time of year in Jerusalem. This year, the event should have started on March 30. They had only four days to sell the artifact and leave the country. Sophia considered the feast to their advantage; the four of them would stand out less surrounded by crowds of starry-eyed European tourists.

Sophia pulled to the side of the forecourt, in front of the air pump. Climbing out of her car, she approached a black Mercedes that was parked to the side, occupying one of the few spaces. A short man, almost a dwarf, leaned on the car. He was dressed in a grey cotton suit. Madison caught up to flank her. Lifen and Odette stayed in their seats.

Sophia stopped in front of the dwarf, saying, "I'm Sophia. I believe you're expecting me."

"You're right on time. My name is Abush," the man smiled, some of his teeth were missing. "I've been told to escort you to our Papa. Any questions?"

"I have no questions. Lead the way, Abush."

Abush-dwarf stepped into his car and pressed to play classical music for the festival: *Their Land Brought forth Frogs.*

. . .

Sophia and her girls were following him to the city of Jerusalem. Even in the late afternoon, it was hot. The old worn-out car they were driving only offered dust and warm air from its air conditioning system. 4ASS women wound down their windows, allowing the wind to play with their hair. The road was a joy: they passed pastoral land at once familiar and foreign —a mix of the rolling hills and rural townships. A racing Yamaha bike merged out of the dense traffic, accelerating up to Abush's car. Sophia gripped the wheel. The adrenaline thrilled through her when she saw how the helmed rider drew a submachine gun. Odette, who sat near Sophia, checked the road behind them. To her terror, two more motorbikes were speeding up through the traffic.

CHAPTER 27

DO OR DIE

"MORE ASSASSINS! Best welcome ever... They're flanking us on bikes! How sweet! I can't maneuver in this dense traffic! Do something! Don't let them draw aim on us!" yelled Sophia.

Lifen, Madison, and Odette drew their guns, waiting for the bikes. Ahead of them, the gunman on the black Yamaha unleashed a crazy rattle of gunfire. Abush braked. He desperately swerved, trying to avoid the rain of bullets. The windows of his car exploded, the bodywork was riddled, full of holes. Abush's car smashed into a neighbouring vehicle, shouldering it aside, then accelerating into a gap. Somehow, the dwarf was still driving. A gunman on a Yamaha followed him. Full of rage, Sophia punched the accelerator, lurching forward, steering to hit the bike. It almost escaped her swing, but she clipped the rear wheel. The bike corkscrewed and crashed to the road. The rider tumbled along. The car behind swallowed him under the tires. Sophia saw the car lurch and bounce as it rode over him before coming to a jaunty halt. The motorcyclist on their left accelerated forward, producing a chromed pistol.

Madison acted quickly—her belt already unbuckled. She

aimed out the open window, which galvanised the assassin; the shots were simultaneous, the back window shattered. Odette screamed, "Va te faire fourte!"

Madison's shots reached the goal and the man folded forward, crashing into a taxi to his left. The taxi slowed down, skidding to a halt with a screech of tires. The third assassin didn't move closer. He took out his gun, firing at Sophia's car. The first bullet punched through the rear passenger door, narrowly missing Odette.

"Shoot him, Oddie!" Lifen screamed. "Shoot him before he kills us!"

Odette squirmed around trying to get a good aim out of the right-hand rear window. She fired wildly, busting a car tire beyond the bike and firing into the air.

The boss of 4ASS scowled. *In a few seconds, there's going to be dead bodies in this car*, Sophia thought to herself. She drew her pistol and held the wheel with her left hand. She aimed backwards, with her gun upside down. The assassin fired again; the seat stuffing exploded next to her head.

Sophia's first shot clipped the rider's shoulder, making him wobble on the bike. She adjusted her aim, focusing with all her will. The second shot bit into his chest. The assassin stiffened and crashed. His Yamaha jumped, mangling the body underneath it.

Madison whooped, "Yeah! What a fucking shot! Don't forget who taught you that!"

"Keep your eyes open for trouble," Sophia growled, then focused on keeping up with Abush's car.

Abush pulled off the highway at the next exit. Sophia followed. Abush stopped behind acacia trees that concealed them from the road. Now, they were amidst fields of corn, which rustled in the breeze. Sophia climbed out of the car, flanked by her followers. The man leaned heavily on the opposite side of the car, drenched in sweat. Blood oozed from his thigh where a bullet had grazed him.

Seeing how rattled he was, Sophia curbed her anger and spoke in an ominous growl, "What was THAT?"

"I don't know. They tried to kill me, too! Papa Zen will know more than I do, but first, we have to get there. I'll take a different route now...," the dwarf answered.

Sophia checked the faces of her companions. They had to decide—to follow or to get back. Lifen shrugged. She always had opinions, a big mouth, and the cold heart of a robot. She spoke, "Papa Zen obviously has enemies, but they might lose interest in us when the business is concluded."

"What about the fact that our cars are filled with bullet holes?" asked Odette.

"She is right. Things won't go smoothly if we are pulled over by the local police," added Madison.

"Don't worry," said the damaged dwarf. "Let me make a phone call."

Sophia looked unsure for a moment, then nodded. She wanted to ask what he meant by that, but it was not the right time to be curious. The four women let him make the call, trying to stay positive.

Wow, our Papa has influence over the police! Madison made a note to herself.

The two cars, still riddled with bullet holes, drove through a tangle of backroads that wound their way amidst the suburbs of Jerusalem. The city was thriving with activity. Everywhere they looked, the Passover festivities asserted its influence: parks were transformed into bustling fares; plazas were cluttered with temporary stalls and entertainers. Million-year-old events created what is today called the Holy Land. In fact, it is a very small place, no more than fifty miles across, located between the river Jordan and the Mediterranean. The fate of many dynasties started there: the first humans passed through on their way to Africa; the magical system of words inspired the growth of many civilizations. This area, the narrow strip of land, helped to develop a social life, something that characterizes our cultures. The concept of God was born here, too: *as the mountains surround Jerusalem, so the LORD surrounds his people, from this time forth and forevermore.*

Sophia linked Jerusalem to the zone where the last battle between the forces of good and evil would take place. She would be happy to die here. She was ready for the inevitable clash of two tough forces: 4ASS and Papa Zen.

Finally, her team had arrived in an old section of the city. Stepping out of the car, the four women found themselves surrounded by old crumbling buildings, small businesses and —on the opposite side of the road—impressive, yet dilapidated cinema. Its windows were boarded shut, and its billboards advertising movies were a decade old. Sophia positioned the ponderous weight of the satchel on her left, bearing the sacred box on its cross strap.

Abush climbed out of his car and walked back to meet them. He had wound a bandage around his leg, but it had soaked through. He walked with a limp.

"Here we are!" he gestured past the trickle of cars at the cinema.

"In that cinema?" Lifen asked.

"It's nicer on the inside, believe me." Abush led them to a small door next to the grand entrance, letting them into the reception. It was abandoned, frozen in time: posters sagged off the walls, velvet couches were covered in dust. Two dark-skinned men were standing in the room. They were dressed in suits and turbans, cradling submachineguns in their hands. Neither spoke. They simply stared at the women as they passed.

"Is anyone else getting a bad feeling? No?" murmured Odette.

"Yeah, they didn't check us. I guess guns are fully allowed in this cinema," Madison chuckled.

Abush led them behind the counter, into a backroom where four local men played cards; pistols on their hips, two assault rifles leaned against a nearby wall.

Sophia didn't like the way the men eyed Lifen's dress. They were humourless, silent, almost glowering. One man with a moustache had a sneer teasing at the corner of his mouth. *Is that sexism, greediness, lust, or do they know something I don't?* Sophia thought to herself.

Abush guided them up a flight of stairs into a small conference hall. Two more swarthy gunmen stood here. The centre of the room was dominated by a long table, draped with a white cloth, laden with bowls of fruit and trays of hors d'oeuvres. The walls were decorated with a jaunty collection of old paintings in antique frames. The brilliant colors and simple imagery of wallpaper gave the impression of harmony and romanticism. The damaged carpet was concealed behind several large Persian rugs. Before Sophia could speak, a door at the far end of the hall burst open; a tall, energetic Black man walked in. He was dressed in a beige silk suit, diamond cufflinks sparkling at his wrists. He was flank by two stone-faced bodyguards in blue dresses. One of them carried a slim silver case. Something vaguely exotic and sinister had filled the hall.

"Sophia von X, *ani meod sameah lirot otha! Ma shlomha?* I heard you were attacked on your commute here. Please, allow me to extend my apologies. The criminals responsible for this act are being hunted down."

Sophia recognized Papa's voice from their conversation in Italy.

"No need to hunt down the ones that did it," said Sophia, taking in each of Papa's movements. "They're already dead."

"I heard that! Tough girls you are... Those men deserved it. Please, sit down. I always like to greet my associates with food and wine. It's hard to be hospitable without hospitality, don't you think?" he gestured at the snacks on the table with emphasis.

Papa sat at the head of the table in a barrel-formed mahogany chair. The broad, heavy seat had an exaggeratedly deep seat-rail, carved with reeded detailing. The machine-woven upholstery showed a red shield with two heads of the snakes.

Papa's bodyguard placed the silver case on the floor by his side. Sophia and her team sat down, too. Papa Zen looked Abush up and down, asking, "Why are you standing there bleeding? Go and get that leg seen to and change your clothes. You will have our guests thinking we are barbarians."

Abush left, flushed with embarrassment. A young, pretty Black woman clad in a long dress, with her hair covered, entered the room. She was bearing a tray with a bottle of wine and five glasses.

"Are you really Papa Zen?" asked Lifen, doubting.

"Yes, in the flesh!"

"Strange, we thought you were from Israel. The business world seems to think you are Jewish," added Odette.

The man showed a broad Hollywood smile, bizarre mischief twinkling in his eyes. He leaned on the back of his chair, telling his story: "I was born in Ethiopia. My father was Ethiopian, but my mother was Jewish. They came back to Israel when I was only seven years old. I studied architecture and economics, then worked as a real estate investment banker in London for several years, before moving back to my roots four years ago. That's when I started my Bible Project... For a long time, Ethiopians have been part of the tapestry of life in this holy city, but we are second class citizens. Or maybe even the third. We are not trusted or treated fairly. I have to admit, I use an actor as a mask. He is my eyes and ears in this country. Of course, he is a Jew. The strategy has proved quite useful, but he is the third mask I have worn so far."

"What happened to the other two?" Madison asked, blown away by the weird conversation.

"Killed, of course. I step on the toes of too many criminals in this city to be safe. I hide in the shadows; it gives me the power behind the throne. Now you see the real me because there would be no point sending an actor to look at your birthmark, Sophia," Papa looked at Sophia with a spark in the eyes.

Sophia frowned. She had forgotten that this man wished to view her birthmark for himself. She had not dressed to show it.

"Why do you want to see it?" Sophia asked.

"According to our reports, Jesus was married. His family moved to the south of France, living in one of the Jewish communities there. We know also that their children moved to Italy. The answer to your 'why' is here...Ready? All descendants of Jesus' family had a birthmark in the form of a cross, on their left shoulder," explained Papa Zen, enjoying the shock on Sophia's face.

The Black girl poured red wine into his glass. He scented the bouquet and nodded, "Ze taaim!" The girl approached the others in the room, pouring the wine. Sophia refused to drink. Odette began to sip.

Madison wrinkled her nose, "No way I'm drinking that! Do you have a beer?" The girl shook her head nervously. Lifen said no to the wine and sat, tensely listening.

"Lifen? Don't you drink, too? Ah, I forgot, you are pregnant! The child of Thomas von Essen, as I heard," Papa Zen dropped the last words in full silence.

Sophia turned to Lifen, only to face her ice-cold expression. Some lies hurt us more than the others; some lies are too toxic to ever be told. Sophia wanted to wail from the enormous growing pain in her chest but decided that the best she could do in this insane situation is to stick to her plan. She had to pretend to be calm, under control; she had to keep her head cool.

"Should we get down to business, Papa?" asked an angry Lifen, taking the glass of red wine from the table. "I'm sure there's plenty of time for small-talk once we are done."

"Why not? why not?!?" said the man in the beige suit. "Have you brought the pages, girls?"

"Yes. I have it here, in the box, with me," Sophia answered.

"Wonderful," he looked to the other men in the room and ordered, "leave us! I do not need protection from our beautiful guests. Make sure no enemy gets in here."

One of the men frowned, "Are you sure, Sir?"

"Yes, I will call you if I need you. Go!"

Sophia studied the interaction. Papa Zen was hard to read: he seemed relaxed and confident, not even minding being questioned by a servant. The bodyguards were stiff, trying to conceal nervousness. Sophia glanced at her companions to see if they had noticed it, too, but if they had, they gave no sign. The four gunmen and the girl with a bottle of wine left the room through the rear door, closing it behind them. Sophia was aware that they were now surrounded by a small army. Papa Zen lifted the silver case onto the table, entered a punch code, and swivelled it to face them. One side was filled with crisp blocks of euro bills, held by thin paper strips. The other side showcased gems stones in zip-locked bags.

"Here is half of your money, in cash and diamonds. Untraceable cash! The rest will be transferred to the same bank account as soon as I see the twelve pages of the Bible with my own eyes. I have taken the liberty of providing the majority in gemstones, as in cash would weigh too heavy for elegant ladies like you four!" he laughed. "Rest assured, all of the gemstones have papers; none of them have been stolen."

Lifen stood and slowly walked over to the open case, examining the contents. She lifted a wad of money, flicking through the notes, scenting them.

Papa Zen looked time to time at Lifen, then his voice cut through the dead air of the room, "It's time to see what God has kept secret for so long, Sophia. Let us open the sacred box to check what I have purchased."

Sophia lifted the satchel onto the table and carefully slid the lead box out of it. Practice and examination had made her an expert of jiggling the tight lid off: she made it look easy. She lay the lid aside as Papa watched her every motion, then she removed a layer of foam, cotton cloth, revealing the uppermost first page of twelve.

Papa Zen bent down to study the first page.

"This does appear to be genuine. Are all the pages here?"

"Yes, yes, everything that was originally in the box when it was uncovered," Sophia nodded.

In that minute, Lifen cleared her throat, mumbling, "The money is fake..."

Sophia studied her worried face, then looked at Papa Zen: the man was genuinely perplexed. He said, "This is not possible, ladies. That money has been drawn straight out of the bank. In any case, there is only twenty-five million in cash. You still have money in your bank account."

Madison rushed to the zipped packages of diamonds. She emptied the bags, checking one by one.

"Seems these diamonds are fake, too. Do you think we're fools?" Madison held up a plastic packet, showing it to Papa Zen.

"That is not true! I will get to the bottom of this... Give me a minute," Papa stood up, slowly moving to the door. At that moment, Lifen started coughing. She stared at her hand; it was speckled with blood. The Asian woman grimaced in pain, staggered to her feet, then doubled over and collapsed on the floor.

"Lin!" shouted Madison, running to her side. "What's wrong? What the hell's going on! She is pregnant, you evil!"

"It's the damn wine," hissed Sophia quickly drawing her pistol and levelling it on Papa's face. "You better have an antidote or I'm going to put a bullet right between your eyes. NOW!"

"This is madness! I...I...," Papa's face twisted in pain. He let out a strangled cry as he fell to his knees and vomited up bile mixed with blood. Staring at the mess around, he stammered, "What is this?!? That madman means to kill us all!"

"Who means to kill us all?" screamed Sophia. She was furious.

Papa Zen stared up from his knees, with bloody drool on

his rich suit, "I'm an actor. I was hired to acquire that box. I thought it was a legitimate deal." He coughed up more blood, grimacing in pain.

Lifen shivered on the floor letting out a scream of agony, blood gurgling between her lips.

"We need to do something! I am next! I've tried that damn wine, too," cried Odette.

"Fuck! We don't know anything about this toxin," said Madison in despair. "What should we do, Boss? They will all die soon!"

The false Papa Zen drew in a shuddering breath and gurgled out more words, "...Berakhiah, Baruch Altschuler hired me. He did this. He wants you dead! The men outside work for him...Ezra!" he tried to continue but began choking on blood, froth and bubbles oozing from his mouth. His pleading eyes were staring up at Sophia; he couldn't say more.

The door opened and two men in blue suits entered the room, pistols drawn. Sophia fired before the men had properly taken in the room. A red hole appeared in the right-hand man's forehead: the back of his head exploded in gore. Seems the hollow tip bullets in her .45 automatic were proving gruesomely effective. The second man fired at Odette but missed. She dove under the table before Madison's .44 magnum revolver barked twice, hitting him in the center of his chest. He collapsed in a lifeless pile. A third man took a quick look around the door frame only to have the top of his head explode in red pulp, his eyes losing focus. The fourth man did not show up.

"We need to get out of this room," said Sophia. She looked one last time at Lifen's body, whispering, "Forgive me, Lin. If we make it out of this mess alive, I promise to punish him."

Sophia stalked down the hall towards the rear door—pistol ready, the Hagia box in the bag behind her back. Madison bundled up a shivering Odette, following to the exit. The false Papa Zen stretched out a pleading hand towards them. His face was a mask of abject horror.

Sophia plucked up one of the assassin's unused guns. She poked the barrel around the corner, firing a burst of wild shots. Following her lead, Madison did the same on the other side of the door. Then she burst into the next room. One more gunman was to her left; he had thrown himself flat on the floor, trying to hide. Sophia shot him in the shoulder from the other angle, helping Madison. The pistol clattered from his nerveless fingers. Sophia drove a knee into the man's face, smashing his nose flat. The gunman recoiled, curling into a ball, clutching his face.

"Where is he? Real Papa?" Sophia yelled, "Where is the sick bitch that poisoned us?"

The man didn't speak. Instead, eyes watering, he lifted himself and lunged desperately for his pistol.

"Look out!" Madison shouted.

Sophia stamped on the gunman's hand as he grasped the pistol, breaking half the bones in his fingers. He screamed in pain, trying to draw it back, but she ground it into the floor with her boot. His eyes rolled back. He fainted.

Madison stared at her Sicilian friend. Sophia's eyes were alight with murder; she was on a rampage. Madison had never been so scared of a person in her life. Pistol in hand, Sophia jerked open the door in the back of the cafeteria, finding a corridor. It was becoming more apparent that only the two rooms behind her had been outfitted for use.

Sophia scanned the cafeteria. The benches that lined each wall had built-in storage cupboards under them. She moved to them, pulling open the doors, looking inside, with her gun ready. Seeing what she was doing, Madison copied her on the opposite side of the room. Four doors later, Sophia found the girl who served the wine, on her belly, trembling. She was staring up at Sophia with pools of fear in her eyes. Sophia dragged the girl out of the cupboard, onto her knees, pressing the gun to her forehead. The girl shivered in terror—the gun metal still hot. Madison lowered Odette's twisting body to the floor, clearing her airway. Odette's breaths gurgled horribly as she tried to get air.

Sophia's face flushed with rage. She pressed the gun into the girl's forehead, hissing, "Where's the antidote to the poison? Tell me right now... Right fuckin' now."

"There isn't one! I don't know! I don't have one!" the girl stammered.

"That's the wrong answer."

"Don't! Please, don't kill me!"

Sophia fired three shots over her head, then pressed the hot gun metal into her cheek. The flesh sizzled. "Where is the cure? How do I stop this bloody hell?!"

"I can't... I don't know!"

Sophia fired two more shots over her head and pressed the hot metal into the already burning circle.

"Last chance. Where?"

"There isn't one! I'm so sorry! I'm so sorry!" blubbered the girl.

"I believe you," said Sophia, despair creeping into her voice. Odette flinched as Sophia pulled the trigger, splattering the floor with the blood and brains. She let the body of the girl topple to the floor.

Madison jumped up and shouted, "More men are coming!"

She pointed her magnum at the door into the meeting hall. An Arabian man shouldered through the door. Another was right behind him. The two women fired, trying to hail them with as much lead as possible. Eight shots barked out. The leading man twisted and fell to the floor, riddled with holes. The second took Sophia's .45 round in the stomach staggered drunkenly into the carpet. A scream escaped Odette's mouth— she writhed and curled in agony. She knew she was the next to die.

"You fucker!" Madison shot the next assassin in the chest, as two more rounds from Sophia bit into his torso. He toppled. Madison stamped on the wound in his stomach. He curled up in agony, then froze: his face changed to the color purple.

A new silhouette appeared for a moment around the entrance—someone pressed his face next to the door, took a quick peek. *There were four men in the lower room when we came in. There's probably one pressed on either side of the door,* thought Sophia, calculating how many more they should kill before escaping the cinema.

Madison covered the doorway, focusing, hoping to fire before the gunmen. Sophia stepped forward, picked up the AK-47, leveled it on the wall just right of the door and fired. The gun thundered for two seconds, chewing the plasterboard wall. Then all fell silent, the heavy thud of a body hit the floor. Pragmatic Sophia picked up the second assault rifle, moving to the other side of the room. She could hear the man hyperventilating. She aimed through the wall. At the same time, a new assassin whirled around the corner, screaming something in Arabic. He fired. Sophia shouted, clutched the side of her head, and staggered back. Madison's revolver barked again, more quietly than before, winging the man's shoulder, and making him stagger. Sophia swivelled the assault rifle and emptied the whole clip into the man's body. It was thunderously loud in the confined space, but she didn't care anymore. His white shirt turned crimson—a mist of blood exploded out of the far side of his body. He collapsed in ruin.

Sophia took a quick look around the door frame, looking for extra gunmen, but found none. She was staring in horror at the torn flesh of hands and legs, lying around in the room. Madison moved closer to Odette, checking her pulse.

"I think she is dead," the American woman whispered.

Sophia fixated on Madison with a hard gaze, saying, "Mad, we can't gun our way out of this city. We'll die here, in Jerusalem..."

Madison looked up at her in disbelief.

"Do not give up!" she said aloud. "Let's see how far we can make it. 4ASS forever!"

CHAPTER 28

BOAT SERVICE

THE TWO WOMEN took several clips for their Glocks but abandoned the assault rifles, which had no spare ammunition. They gathered at the door to the stairs. Sophia decided to gun her way out the front. She wanted to use their car to get away. Time was likely running out. Sophia was aware that Papa Zen influenced the police. The police force could be here any second.

"There are two men downstairs, with submachine guns," Madison said. "There is no safe way to go out through the front. Let's just go out the back, point a gun at any car, and take it."

"I hear you," Sophia replied. "My gut is telling me to go through, not away! That's the way we're doing it. I've got a contingency, but timing is important."

"What's the plan?" Madison stammered.

"I don't have time to talk you through it. Follow my lead."

With that, Sophia stepped out onto the stairwell, making her way down as quietly as possible. Madison covered her from the top. They moved slowly, step by step. Sophia was almost at the bottom of the stairs when she heard the gunman. He spun around the corner. Sophia fired. The submachine gun in the assassin's hands exploded. The man swore, his eyes widened as Sophia leveled the gun on his head, saying, "Click!"

The gunman lunged forward, plunged a fist at the woman's belly, and much to his surprise, bounced off hard muscles with little effect.

I've got the high ground; if I jump and knock him on his back, I'll be on top of him and able to finish this fight quickly, Sophia decided.

She sprang at the man before he could understand what she was planning, driving him off his feet. She straddled his torso, ready to pummel his face. On the other side of the room, the second guard stood in the doorway, pointing his weapon at her. Sophia's eyes widened in hatred. The man under her legs struggled to roll her over, to break out of her domination. She let him. He rolled on top of her, clawing his way up so that he could sit astride her. Sophia knew the maneuver well. She gripped him tight with her legs.

Madison moved down the stairs, shouting, "Give me a clear shot!"

At the same time, the gunman in the door shouted in Arabic. Sophia grabbed her assailant's face, squeezing her thumbs into his eyes. He let out a shriek. The man at the door ran forward, clearly intending to shoot Sophia at point-blank range but stumbled into Madison's line of sight. Before he could even raise his hand, his head had taken three bullets.

Sophia twisted her torso, rolling on top of the screaming opponent. She pulled her hands back, driving her right elbow down into his face. He did not parry—his almost blind, bleeding eyes did not see it coming. The first blow stunned him, the second and third left him limp.

"Good work!" said Madison.

"Why waste ammunition, right?" smiled Sophia, staggering up to her feet, breathing raggedly. She reloaded her pistol.

The two cautious figures moved into the front foyer. No one was there.

Wow. Did we kill them all? Madison wondered.

Sophia tried to look nonchalant as she jaywalked through the traffic to her car. She tossed the bag with the box onto the back seat, climbed in, and started the engine. Soon, the two women were driving through the ancient city.

"It's only a matter of time before the cops find us," Madison chewed her lip. "We need to change the car!"

"No. Not this time, Mad," said Sophia, "We're only one hour from freedom. Remember, it hasn't been long. The cops are probably informed to ignore this particular car. The city is in the middle of the feast, too. Plus, they don't know where we're going."

"This time, we're testing our luck for real," Madison added.

Sophia drove west through the city while Madison scrutinized the traffic around them for assassins. Despite their paranoia, they failed to spy a dark green Volvo, following them at a distance.

They successfully escaped the city, turning to the road leading to the coast. Sophia pulled the car up at a car park near Port of Jaffa. She left the keys in the ignition, speaking to Madison, "Bring your bag. Add anything we need from Lifen's or Odette's gear."

Madison grimaced but did as she was told. She still couldn't believe the 4ASS team was gone. Carrying their bags, the two women trudged down the road lined with stones. A yacht glowed on the shadowy waters of the Mediterranean Sea; a couple of tiny figures wandered on the deck. Sophia and Madison rounded a rocky outcrop. They came straight to a speedboat nestled at the edge of the surf. A blonde man in a blooming Hawaiian shirt sat on the bench, mesmerized by his smartphone. Madison noticed a slank woman with pink hair, wading in the shallows, kicking up water.

Sophia said to the woman, "Hi, Grace. This is Madison. One of the friends I told you about. Mad, this is Grace."

"Hi, Sabina," Grace said cheerily. "Where're your other friends?"

The smile faded from Sophia's face for a moment. She glanced down at the ground, "They decided to stay here. They met cute guys...you know how it is."

Madison was surprised that Grace didn't seem to pick up on Sophia's lie. She smiled and said, "Cool, I hope that works out for them! Are you guys good to go? Sven is chapping at the bit." She gestured over to the blonde man who still hadn't noticed they were there.

"Yeah, we're good to go any time you are. I just need to get back to the car. I forgot to leave a surprise for the girls. They are going to pick up the car later on..." Sophia winked to pop-eyed Madison. She left in a hurry.

Grace ambled over to Sven, waving her hand between him and his phone. He turned his eyes up, "Woah, Grace. Did you know that dolphins have a complex language? They are smarter than us, humans!"

"Yes! I did."

"Cool, huh?"

"Sabina is here, Honey. We can go."

Sven climbed up to his feet, proving to be tall like a tower,

"Awesome! This place sucks. Why are we even here? Cyprus was more fun…"

"Sabina needed to pick up her friends. Don't you remember?" Grace kissed Sven on the cheek.

"Oh, yeah! Woah, sexy friend. Is it Sabina?" he gave Madison a dopey grin.

"Don't be a chauvinist," grouched Grace. "How many lines of coke did you do before you came out here? You're like a zombie of the flirt, Sven. Sabina had to get back to her car. This is Madison, by the way…"

"I don't know. Whatever, fuck. Let's go," Sven waded out to the speedboat, climbed aboard in a tangle of limbs, followed by the two girls.

Sophia showed up near the boat right on time. Madison helped her get on board. Cocaine didn't seem to affect Sven's ability to drive.

The girls realized they were heading to the power yacht they'd seen earlier from the coastal park. The boat pulled up at rear stares. Two wiry boys jumped on the speedboat. They started attaching cables with a small crane rig, trying to winch it up onto the deck. Sophia and Madison climbed on board. Grace gave them a tour because Sven crumpled into the first chair he found and continued staring at his phone.

The ship was beautiful: an expensive luxury yacht with private rooms, a crew of young guys, and relaxing pretty girls. Grace showed the rooms and then left in search of Sven. In the comfort of the chamber, which was clean, apart from some lacey underwear on the bed that Madison tossed outside, Sophia finally answered her questions. She explained how she'd reconnected with Grace, asking for getaway help. Grace had influence over the man with the boat. Sophia had talked her into pressuring Sven into spending a week at Jerusalem. Sven Orazi was a toy boy millionaire. He owed Grace a great deal of money for cocaine, so she was living off him, traveling the world. They were also an item, as much as either of them was capable.

Only when the yacht started slowly cruising towards international waters did Sophia allow herself to relax a little. *We made it...even if Lifen, her baby and Odette didn't. This can still work. I'll contact the Mafia and sell the lost pages that way,* Sophia thought to herself.

Most of the crew, together with Grace, were partying in the main living room: playing spin the bottle, snorting lines of cocaine, dancing to heavy music. The mainland was behind them. They slowly cruised into international waters. The sea was mercifully calm. Neither Madison nor Sophia could sleep —haunted by the horrors of the day. Madison had taken advantage of the free alcohol on board, drowning her sorrows in rum.

Sophia stood at the prow. She grasped the rail and tilted her face up at the stars, letting the warm sea breeze lull away her worries. She studied the sky, wondering what she should have done differently. She blamed herself and her unprofessionalism for the deaths of two from her super team.

———

Madison was drunk. She stood up from her bed, pushing away a stoned Sven, who had been trying to get into her pants all evening, promising to lick her like a rabbit. She headed out, telling him, "Sophia has been on the deck for hours. I should check if she's okay."

C H A P T E R 29

—————

T H E L A S T S O N G

T HE SMALL BOAT slid silently up behind the massive yacht. It had taken hours to catch up with the vessel, but now they were close. The lack of people on the deck and the loud music made the final approach very simple. Mahound jumped onto the stairs that ascended from the water, making his way to the deck. It was abandoned. He slipped from cover to cover, using piles of rope and furniture, to conceal his form. The control cabin was empty, too. *These crazy bastards are just letting the yacht wander the sea*, he thought to himself.

He moved past the cabin, to the foredeck. A lone figure in a gown stood at the furthest tip of the deck—her brown hair tousled in the wind. Mahound narrowed his eyes, thinking, *this might be my lucky day. That might be her...*

He stepped forward. One more woman walked into his view. She paused, then started walking towards the girl on the prow. It was a tall woman with platinum blonde hair, bare feet, wearing black panties and a black bra.

"That's one of them—the woman called Madison. American...two birds with one stone," Mahound whispered, smiling.

For a moment, he considered shooting her, but it wasn't necessary. She was unarmed and drunk. He slipped up behind her, unwinding a wire garotte, then smoothly looped it over her head. He yanked the handles, pulling her back against him, lifting her body so that she couldn't get proper traction on the ground. Madison's eyes bulged as the wire garotte bit into her neck, cutting flesh and crushing her veins. She kicked her legs, trying to grasp the wire, but a few seconds later, her vision shrank. She went black—the blood to her brain was cut off.

Mahound was happy. He lowered her body to the deck. Her legs gave odd little twitches. He had seen it before—it was the movement of a panicked body, coming to grips with the fact that it was dead. He put away his garotte, approaching Sophia's figure.

Mahound drew his pistol and spun on a silencer. The click of it caught Sophia's ear. When she turned, the unknown man in black stood before her, holding a gun. Sophia could see Madison's sprawled form behind him. She stared; her heart pounding in her chest.

"Who are you?" the Sicilian woman asked.

Mahound pulled off his balaclava. Sophia gasped as she saw the sullen face marked by a deep winding scar and a black eyepatch.

"It's you…The Ripper! The man who tried to kill me in Germany."

"The last you'll see, Sophia von X."

"Why haven't you killed me yet?"

"I've been sent by someone who doesn't want the missing pages you discovered to see the light of day. They want them burned. The code is too dangerous for people to know."

"Do you want to know about the code? That's why you didn't shoot me in the back," guessed Sophia.

"Yes, but it doesn't save you."

"I'll tell you everything if you tell me your name. I want to know the name of my murderer."

"You still think you'll live after this? You won't, bitch. My name is Mahound. Now tell me about the box."

Sophia took a deep breath. The box was on board, but the twelfth page had been left in Israel, in safe hands. She prepared to lie, "It speaks of religion, both righteous, peace-loving, and wrathful to those who defy its truth," she paused.

"Continue...," Mahound said.

"It clearly shows that the second Messiah is on the way. He is coming to show that modern religions are a pure invention of humans, who twisted God's teachings to create compliant sheep-like flocks. It also explains the symbolic language behind the Book of Revelation: seven lamps, twelve angels, one 140,000 who are waiting in Heaven..."

"Okay. Okay. I'm tired of this bullshit. Goodbye."

"Don't you want to know more, Mr. Mahound?" Sophia gazed at him.

"Well, the rapture doesn't arrive until the word of the Lord is heard in every corner of the world. You are defying the will of God if you destroy them."

"You've let a dead man like Jesus get into your head, girl." The man with the scar shook his head.

"You can't kill me. I have a covenant with God; he is my... friend. I saw him in the Hagia Sophia. Do you see the cross on my shoulder? This is the birthmark of Jesus. He said, when we are weak, we are strong, and I believe in it." Sophia looked behind the assassin, in hopes of seeing any living soul on deck.

"If that's so, you've got nothing to fear. I'll tell you what, if these bullets bounce off you, then I'll follow you to the end of the earth. I'll help you spread the word myself," he said as he stood laughing at her.

"Can I ask who hired you? Please, this is my last wish."

"I don't know her name. She was French."

Three shots barked out, cutting deep into Sophia's chest. She staggered back, shocked by pain. Then, losing her balance, she pitched over the railing and fell into the sea. She had vanished by the time Mahound reached the rail.

CHAPTER 30

BARUCH'S WOMAN

A FIGURE SAT SUNKEN in an armchair, lit only by the glow of a television. On the seventy-five-inch screen, a news reporter in a black suit strove towards a handsome young Jewish man, surrounded by two bodyguards, pushing aside the public and reporters alike.

The reporter spoke, "Mr. Altschuler...Mr. Berakhiah Altschuler! It's me, Henry Whistler, from *Jerusalem Today*. I've interviewed you a couple of times before. Would you be able to answer a few questions?"

The young man stopped, "I could answer a few questions, but make it brief. I have a meeting to attend at the Church of St. Anne."

"Thanks, Mr. Altschuler. Is there any truth to the claims that you have had dealings with the dangerous American-Italian criminal organization 4ASS?"

Berakhiah looked serious as the wavering camera focused on his aquiline features. He answered, "That is a baseless claim! A fabrication of my detractors and political enemies. For obvious reasons, they want me to fail. They want Israel to fail."

"Do you think these rumors will affect your campaign to become the next prime minister?" the reporter asked.

"Not at all. My true followers know I would never deal with criminals. I have chosen to step out of the business world and run for office to do the exact opposite—to restore dignity and peace to the streets of Jerusalem. That's all I have time for today..." The Jewish man added to the camera, "Plus, I would never harm such beautiful ladies."

"The last question. Is there any truth to the rumors that the Hagia Sophia robbery is linked to the lost pages of the Bible and your name? Did you order to kill Sophia von X and her team? Where're those sacred pages now?" the questions poured down without regrets from the reporter's mouth.

Berakhiah kept moving forward, repeating, "No comments."

A nasty journalist and the cameraman followed him. The young politician climbed into a black car saloon with tinted windows that rode low on its suspension.

The figure in the armchair pressed a button on the remote, changing the channel. The woman who stood behind him switched off the screen. She was slim, with short curly hair. She leaned forward, kissing the man who watched TV.

"I'll find her, *mon amour*—her and the last page. I promise," the woman hissed through her teeth in a French accent. She went out of the dark room, leaving the man alone in the shadows of his thoughts.

In the light of the day, you could see that the woman was Odette. The only difference in her usual outfit were her eyes: icy, distant, and sinister.

CHAPTER 31

———

BLOODY BAY

THE FIRST THING she saw when she opened her eyes was
the fantastic blue hues of the water and the waves which looked
serene. She was lying on the big terrace of the beach house,
surrounded by almond trees lined up with giant pink magnolias to provide shade. Dr. Pablo Garcia sat on a chair, talking
with someone on the phone. He stood up and ended the call
when he saw that Sophia had awakened.

"How do you feel, Sophia? I've been worried you'd get
worse after the flight."

"Alive... The last thing I remember is that somebody shot
me on the yacht not so far from Jerusalem. Where are we
now?"

Dr. Garcia nodded. "True, Grace helped me get your body
out of the water. I followed you on the boat just as we
agreed..." He waved vaguely to the beach. "Foxy, my old friend,
owns a beach-front home here in Tobago. He assisted me in
getting you to Bloody Bay safely... as a dead body, of course. I
mean, we transferred you here in a coffin. You are dead to the

world outside, Sophia. Do you need anything? Water? Hungry?"

"No, maybe that lemonade on the table." Sophia watched Dr. Pablo Garcia walk to the table and pour an orange drink into a glass. It was a bit of an awkward situation – she was surrounded by people she barely knew, who had shifted her as a dead body on a private plane to the Caribbean. But she assumed it was for the best. "So, what now, Pablo?"

"First of all, you have to rest, and then we'll plan our next steps." He sounded exhausted.

Sophia fidgeted for a moment. "What about your Foxy friend? He can get into a lot of trouble because of my stay here."

"Don't worry, Sophia, Foxy is my boyfriend. His real name is Frederick, but friends call him Foxy because he can get away with anything and escape any situation..."

A young Indian woman entered the terrace. Her smile shone brighter than the sun. "My name is Kashvi, or Kash if you like."

Sophia smiled and said in return, "hello, Kash," as she drank some more lemonade, trying to understand her actual role here: was she a prisoner or a guest?

"The document is ready, Pablo. Did you tell Sophia about seven messengers?" Kash had beautiful long, dark hair that reflected on the sun and looked almost entirely colorless, like mist.

Sophia glanced at her over the rim of her glass. She was jittery with nerves and her stomach rebelled after that drink Pablo had poured her.

"What is it? What's going on? Why do you do everything behind my back?" Sophia tried to stand up but didn't have enough strength to support her body yet.

"Because you need rest, but you are right, Sophia. To make it short, the last page tells us that there are seven messengers with the birthmark of Jesus, the special cross just like yours."

"Or mine," added Kash.

"Do you have it too?" Sophia was surprised. She had never met anyone who had a similar cross birthmark. Kash was wearing a bathrobe with green leaves and flowers on the back. She dropped it to one side and showed a birthmark on her left shoulder.

"Well, all seven messengers have to die... at least some way or another. It's some kind of purification, as I told you before when we first spoke on the phone," Dr. Pablo explained.

"Sure, I remember. And I almost died."

"I think it doesn't count, Sophia," he sighed.

Kash clarified: "Pablo wants to say that you must be dead for some time; otherwise, it doesn't count. I was dead for an hour, and I got back. You were shot and unconscious with the help of the medication. It's a different thing."

"Hm, you lost me... Do you mean I have to die again?"

"Yes. When all seven are reborn, we can proceed to the next phase."

Kashvi came closer and sat on the chair beside Sophia. She looked at her for a few seconds, then leaned forward and kissed her forehead. The movement frightened Sophia, but she didn't show it. Pablo watched the scene in silence, and when Kashvi stood up and walked inside the house, he reassured, "we are on your side, Sophia. Remember, it was you who asked me for help."

"I appreciate everything you've done, Pablo. But I would really like to find the people who tried to kill me."

Dr. Garcia was silent for a long moment, staring at his hands. "Well, I'll help you if you'll help me."

"Continue... What is the next phase?" Sophia muttered.

"To get our hands on the salphinx."

"What is that?" Sophia asked, perplexed. She didn't trust Dr. Garcia. She stretched out her legs and checked the door and the empty beach behind the magnolias, just in case. The right-side view of the beach was breathtaking, with intricate rocks and verdant forest lines covering them.

"It's a kind of trumpet from Ancient Greece. We need it because we have to exchange it against rkan-dun," Dr. Garcia explained. He took an iPad from the table and showed her a black-and-white picture of a strange horn resembling a speaker. "Rkan-dun is some kind of trumpet made of human bones. Foxy - I mean Frederick - thinks that Professor Savelsberg keeps it in his private collection in Stockholm, Sweden."

"And how do we get that salphinx?" Sophia asked.

"That's where the problem lies. It's displayed in Boston's Museum of Fine Arts. We have to steal it."

"No, no, no, I can't!"

"Look at the bright side; what if this is where you will die?" Kash smiled. She was standing near the doorframe again, watching.

Pablo chuckled. "Kash, you have to learn how to talk to people. You'll scare Sophia, and we need her." He was irritated.

"Ah, please, stop telling me what to do. You are not my father," Kash hissed.

The whole situation – especially the last conversation – reminded Sophia of mayhem in a children's playground.

"Do you think it's funny?" Sophia gasped for air. Her head ached and she couldn't breathe from sudden anger.

"We can't change anything. We have to do what we have to do. This is a prophecy; this is how we'll crack the code of the twelfth page," Dr. Garcia replied.

"By stealing some old trumpet? Are you kidding me?" Sophia laughed in anger.

"Yes. By following the revelation of the twelfth page, by following your path."

Sophia grimaced. "Whatever... I'm tired, Pablo. I want to shower, and then I need to sleep."

"You have nothing to fear from us," Kash said, looking at the sky, where dark clouds were moving quickly toward the house. "Let's go inside, dear... The storm is on its way."

They stood in the spacious living room that looked like it was out of a magazine.

"This way." Dr. Pablo Garcia took the stairs, and Sophia followed him. "This staircase was designed in the 18th century by Alexander Koping-Strauss to evoke the feeling of being outside."

Sophia nodded. The use of white paint on the walls and the absence of any private photos or paintings combined with a black stair made of marble gave the sense of an airy yet unpleasant space. Dr. Garcia opened the first door to the left. The bedroom was large, bright, and luxurious but just as impersonal as the rest of the house.

"If you need anything, just shout. There is a bathroom behind the door. If you have a problem with anything, just let me know." He paused. "We have plenty of time."

The last words sounded fake; Sophia didn't believe him. After the door closed behind her, she collapsed onto the bed, making crazy plans about running away from Doctor Madness and his team. She tried to fall asleep but couldn't. She blankly stared at the ceiling, thinking about her mother and how much she wanted to see her, when someone knocked on the door. It was Kashvi.

"Pablo and Frederick are going out. They plan to hide the twelfth page where nobody will ever find it. It would be best to follow them. What do you think?"

"Hide where? In Tobago?"

"Maybe. But I'm pretty sure they're hiding the document somewhere in the sea. They're going to leave in a few minutes. Let's change and go after them, yes?"

"Why can't we go *with* them?" Sophia asked with suspicion.

"We can try... "

Sophia changed clothes and walked downstairs. Two men, Pablo and Frederick, were arguing. They went quiet as soon as they noticed the presence of their guest.

"Sophia, what's wrong? You shouldn't be up!" Dr. Garcia sounded concerned.

"What are you fighting about?" Sophia looked at Frederick – or Foxy – who reminded her of Thomas von Essen.

"Nothing. Going through the details for the preparation of the biggest heist in history. Right, mate?" Fredrick winked at Dr. Garcia.

Epilogue

January 1, 2019

TO: realuckolifebelt22784@gmail.com
FROM: dgarcia4everX@gmail.com
SUBJECT: I can't walk on water, but here I am

Hola Ucko!

I know I haven't been in touch for a very long time. My life moves on too quickly, and if I don't keep up, I get dragged... As you know, I've been badly ill, but I'm recovering. Luckily, there's a great doctor here, Mr. Pablo San Isidro.

I can't tell you where I am, but tell all my friends that I'm safe: surrounded by engraved rocks, books, horses, and 'open-air' art. I sent the letter to your post box at the university. It is my new novel about *things that matter*. Each chapter (there're 12) is a riddle that offers a unique insight into the temple of peace, the excellent harbor of biblical knowledge, the power of everlasting love. Please, keep it safe. If I don't contact you next month, publish it online. Spread the word, Ucko. The world will be grateful.

Adios!

Your friend, Garcia xxxx

January 2, 2019

TO: *dgarcia4everX@gmail.com*
FROM: *realuckolifebelt22784@gmail.com*
SUBJECT: *When we are weak, we are strong*

Hi, Garcia!

Glad to hear you are feeling better. I knew you'd survive your flu or whatever it was. Do you remember Mr. Cassidy from the faculty of Geography, the one with a bushy brown beard? He loved photography, guns and young pretty girls... too much. Well, he is dead. Killed by local Mafia. I think he was dealing drugs on the side, and something went wrong. I just wanted to mention it, thinking it would make you happy. You were always the righteous one, fighting against evil. At least this is how your friends remember you.

Feel free to send me any novel you wish. I'd be delighted to help. Say hi to Mr. Pablo San Isidro from me.

Take care,

Your friend, Ucko xxxx

About the Author

"Witty dialogue and unique, often surprising twists and turns." — Louise Rizolli, Blåsbo Publisher's SE.

Victoria Ray is a Silver Medal Winner of the Reader's Favorite Contest. She is a recipient of the National Reader's Choice, Black Orchid, Best Indie, Book Excellence Award, Grindstone Literary, and Reader's Views Literary Awards, among others. Ray lived in different places worldwide before returning to her favorite place on the planet: Sweden. When she is not writing absurd stories or fast-paced, versatile thrillers featuring a trail of endless bodies and brave women, Victoria enjoys reading, baking bread, yoga, and traveling.

Follow author:
BLOG - Raynotbradbury.Blog

Acknowledgments

For patience and guidance, I would like to thank H. M. Ohlsson, Anna Moe, and K.E. Garland from Writing Endeavors®, along with Sabina Gabrielli Carrara, for lending her first name to the hero of this book.

I'd like to express my deep appreciation to all my followers: on the blog RayNotBradbury (WordPress) and to my family, for supporting all of my early ideas, thoughts, stories, and heroes without question, which gave me the freedom to experiment with the writing style and also gave me a huge motivation to publish my first thriller.

For any mistakes (or typos) that remain in this book, I take sole responsibility.

Almost Faithful

One broken woman
Two ordinary families
Three dangerous men

Margo and Barry are living the perfect life. They're happily married (or so it seems), working great jobs, and traveling the world. Ellen and David have it all — the looks, the big house by the beach, a successful business, a grown-up daughter, Marie. But underneath, each couple is in crisis, and there is only *one cause.* His name is Charlie.

Charlie is a man with exceptional acting skills, struggling to forget his painful past. A man who is not ready to let go, who is breaking two families and destroying their trust.

Out of options and with their backs against the wall, Margo, Ellen, Marie, and David discover that murder isn't a tool reserved only for criminals...

Are they ready to go to the end?
How easy is it — to take a human life?

Everything changes the moment when the bodies of Ellen and Marie are found dead in their bedrooms. Full of shock, anger, and grief, blaming himself while hiding from the local police, David chooses the dangerous road of revenge: he plans to find Charlie's mysterious boss. The boss is a woman called Pitaya — the reason for all David's troubles.

Little by little, the walls of the seemingly happy, rich, and famous families fall down, and the life of Pitaya, as well as the freedom of David, comes to an end.

Read More - Amazon Store: Victoria Ray